Slow Time

Antje M. Rauwerda

SPUYTEN DUYVIL
NEW YORK CITY

I have a sky blue eye, a grass green, and a dirt brown one, sometimes stony grey.

I have seen this land, the rolling hill, the York Road, Pratt's estate all along Woodbourne Avenue, and his big house Tivoli. Govanstown, Radnor-Winston, Kernewood.

I am beneath. I underpin. I subtend, extend below. All that is connected core-deep, tectonic geologic metamorphic and slow, connected to slow time and the whole of it all.

I have watched Govane parcel up the gifts Lord Calvert gave him and Walters breeding Percheron horses. I have seen the shacks of the poor who worked for the rich. I have seen my fallen pines turned into boards, my oaks turned to handsome wood veneers. I have watched my trees cede to open grass clipped low with great effort, my chicory weeded away and replaced by greenhouses full of lilies, carnations, and roses.

I know the Ulery hotel, the restaurants and car repair businesses along gasoline alley. I have watched the porches sag, the roadways pit and crack. I have seen the people get poorer. They have changed their clothes, the loudness of their religious devotions, and their skin color. I have seen them born and dead.

I know who they have buried with stones on their

heads. I know the small body hidden like an acorn in a tree, in the air, caught in an infelicitous drift. I know, I feel, the empty place where one of them has died but has found no space in my earthen heart.

I have time. I wait, I keep a space.

A sweetgum boy, and his chestnut baby sister. I know how she died.

There will be no peace until the dead child is laid at my heart, with a stone to weigh her home. That death swells beyond the surviving darksad brother, all grown now but never reaching past his guilty conscience. What happened is a disturbance in the soul of my landscape, an unease, an unrest. It spreads from the tall wood and stone house in the old river valley up to the hills, leaching across the York Road.

Others who live in contact with my disturbed earth feel it in their feet, their bones, like a magnetic pull to a problem they cannot decipher but spend their whole lives worrying at until it is done.

In parallel, moonbright boy, grey-eyed sister: another branch, but all connected tree limb trunk root earth.

Sweet sweet, gentle now. I see how to resolve it, the sadness of that falling baby.

I see who, and over my skin what paths must cross, to calm it all. I know who I must bring close. The dark boy, of course. He has flown wide, but then back like a haunting crow landing in a fall oak tree. Also, the living grey-eyed sister. She too went far, and was swept by her heart's wind back to this place. Eventually she will feel her way into the roots of it all. I carry them, hold them both.

I place the stories of these people into their wholeness.

As I round the corner out of Rat Alley #2, he's there again, on the porch of the brick row house despite the sun and the roar of Coldspring's afternoon traffic.

"Hey, Miss Em!" as he stands, tall and thin in his shades with a beach hat on his head.

"Hey, Danny! How you doing?"

"Good, good. How's the dogs?"

Blue and Girlfriend are straining in different directions; one towards the thunderous traffic, the other towards a ketchup-stained Popeye's Chicken takeout container lying on Danny's lawn.

"Good, thanks. It's hot in the sun!"

It's hard to hear his response over the traffic noise, so I smile and haul the dogs back onto the sidewalk and start walking up the block. I am only part irritated, which is surprising. Most people who interrupt my solitude, slow down my dog walk, just really annoy me. Not Danny though. I am genuinely smiling as I walk away. He reminds me of Will, my addict half-brother, but more than that I *just like Danny*. It's not romantic or erotic; I'm not into guys.

From my bedroom window, I can hear other folks on the street call out greetings to him at all hours of the afternoon and night, flotsam from the bars and bodegas on York Road, exhausted drunk men and women who wind up on his porch, talking loudly at him while he smiles and nods and listens. I know Danny's probably on the hustle, maybe dealing, this guy who knows everyone. That's biased of me. Not all black guys are dealers. But what's he doing out there all those hours? Why does everyone go talk to him? Ultimately, I don't care. I like Danny. I have a good feeling. Irrational. Over many people I know better, I trust him, this thin black man watching and working the block with his big smile, his huge, long fingered hands held up as he waves his greetings. Our brief conversations make me happy.

I haul the dogs up the block, past the house owned by the two industrious Chinese ladies who've turned their front yard into a sunflower and kale garden, have solar panels on the roof and weed whack their fenced and hidden backyard seemingly constantly, turn onto Kerneway, walk into the relief of the shade trees and then I'm home. Girlfriend isn't the most reliable in the house-training department and she didn't poop on the walk, so even though we've just come in, I let her out back into the yard while Blue, big, droopy and smelling like wet worms more than bloodhound, collapses heavily on the kitchen linoleum to try and catch its cool.

I pour myself a glass of water to drink while I wait for Girlfriend's bark that she's ready to come in, and sit down at the breakfast bar with its white wicker stools. The kitchen still has most of the detailing from my mother's kitchen remodel.

It's a surprise to me to have wound up in Baltimore, in my childhood house no less. I was raised here in Kernewood, an obscure neighborhood between Guilford and Radnor-Winston, with Loyola University on its western side and York Road on its east. York Road is, and I gather always has been, a busy transit street, more about where you're going than about why you're staying put. At least that was mostly true until the methadone clinics came. Now there are destinations here, and counter-intuitively a pretty visible drug trade has sprung up too: as my friend Bev put it "of *course* there're people dealing drugs. Where there's a methadone clinic there's a ready market of vulnerable, needy people wanting them."

Girlfriend should have barked by now. I go to the back door and lean out, looking for her. The backyard is bigger than you'd guess from the small front of the house which is still, legacy of my dentist-dad, tidy and devoid of eccentricity. The green lawn slopes down away from the house, and extends out like a slice of pie with the house at the center. Towards the north side it has a tall black walnut and two dogwoods, one that blooms pink in the spring, the other white; the three mature trees throw big patches of shade.

Deep in the farthest corner from the house is a small dell, an indentation like a bowl, perhaps the remnant of some long-ago stump removal that was never levelled. From the house and patio you can hardly tell the indentation, wide as a small car, deep as a wading pool, is there, but when I was a child it used to be a favorite spot to hide. To lie flat in "the sacred hiding spot," as my brother (my half-brother really) and I used to, would mean being invisible to anyone looking from the house.

Just by the back door is a cement and stone paved area which is good for grilling or sitting outside on the old metal patio furniture when the mosquitos aren't too bad. The yard has a good chain-link fence to keep the dogs in (my addition) and a pretty wrought iron gate which doesn't match the chain-link but was made by an old friend of mine. It's handy if you want to cut through the side garden to get to the front of the house or the street. There's no garage, so my Hyundai is always out on Kerneway, and these days I just leave it unlocked. It's easier to have people rifle through my cds and scraps of paper than to have them break a window to get in. There's iNothing in there: no electronics or cash.

Right now, the gate is open when it should be shut. I had assumed it was shut. *Damn.*

I notice two things: the grill is gone (*Fuckers! Someone stole my frikkin' grill. Jesus Fucking Christ*) and the little dog is not in the yard.

Cold stomach falling down towards my ankles.

Don't panic. She's probably just out front looking for the wild rabbits. I shut the back door, keeping Blue inside, safe. He barks once, deeply, in indignation. Then I jog round to the gate and look through. No sign. I run up to the street. No sign.

Oh shitshitshitshit. Back into the yard to look into the overgrowth past the fence. No sign.

I start calling Girlfriend's name and my heart's racing. I had been inside for how long? At least twenty minutes, probably longer. If she'd noticed the open gate right away, the dog could have gone a long way. Hopefully she hadn't noticed it right away. What if she went to Coldspring and got spooked? Or York? Christ. York Road mid-afternoon is like a cross between bumper cars and the highway.

I start to run, stopping at Coldspring. Did she even come this way? Which way to go next?

"Hey! Miss Em! Miss Em!" It's Danny, come down from his porch onto the sidewalk. "Your little brown dog get out?"

"Yes!" I am breathless and running towards him. "Where'd she go?"

Danny gestures up the alley. "I was trying to find something to tempt her up here to me, but then she jumped and ran!"

I start to run up the alley, my blundstones heavy, slow and thumping, like that dream where there's a tornado coming and you can't run fast enough to get into the shelter in time. Danny shambles behind me, his shuffling jog surprisingly fast, maybe because his legs are so long.

The alley spits out onto Charter Oak. You can see York Road to the right and sure enough, there're cars honking and swerving as Girlfriend veers diagonally across four lanes of traffic. I am cringing trying not to see her get hit by a car. Then I need to cross and I dodge cars recklessly, just trying to keep my eye on her.

She trots down Radnor, through the pot-holed intersection with *Old* York (no traffic). She's got her tail up and is trotting cheerfully. She doesn't look scared. Her trot is still a lot faster than my increasingly out-of-breath jog. I lose sight of her behind some overgrown boxwood hedge. I keep running down the hill and get to Alhambra Ave where it travels low like a river in a narrow valley. And there she is. Sitting, tongue lolling wide and long. She's dripping fat splotches of saliva on the shaded and overgrown concrete steps of a boarded-up house. She's smiling a toothy dog-smile as I get closer, giving me a tired, limp tail wag. Then I get to her, scratching her ears and scolding her in my happy voice because if she hears the anger-panic in me she might up and run from it.

"You silly little bitch." I scold, cheerfully, working the profane pun for some release of my own anxiety. "You are a naughty, sweaty, quick little *bitch* of a Girlfriend."

I am glad she's stopped running and am wondering why I didn't have the presence of mind to bring her leash because now I'll have to either walk home hunched over so I can hold her collar or carry her. I settle on carrying, but first a moment to rest and try to get my breathing back to normal. Girlfriend lies down heavily. She's done running for now.

"Whoa, Nelly!" It's Danny catching up, walking fast and breathing hard. "You got her!"

"Yup!" I'm so happy that I trust Girlfriend not to move for a second and go give him a big hug, the sweat-dark back of his shirt making my hands moist, my sweatier face briefly leaving a dark spot on his T-shirt's shoulder.

"Know where you are, Miss Em?" he asks, taking off his sunglasses and wiping his face with his sleeve. I shake my head.

"Right outside my Ma's house!"

Sweet sweet, gentle soft now. No need to rush it. There they are. Give them time.

"Your Mom's House?" I ask, turning to look up the steps to the boarded up French doors. They are in deep shade under a sagging porch roof supported by what had once been, from the faded paint on them, prettily decorated posts with rounded curves and crown molding. There's a pair of rectangular windows on the middle floor like eyes and a little cracked upstairs window in the attic. I see falling shingles and peeling pale blue paint, a sag to the roof gables's lines. "She doesn't live here anymore, huh?"

Danny's already put his sunglasses back on. "No, Miss Em, she died a long ways back. The big C."

"Just call me 'Em,' I'm not really a 'Miss' kinda person. I'm sorry about your Mom. How long has the house been empty like that?"

"Almost twenty years now!" Danny says, as though he's surprised about it.

"You get squatters?"

"Nah. Boards keep 'em out, and there're nicer places to break into around here anyways. I guess I should check in there sometime for squirrels though." Over the reflective shine of his sunglasses, I can see he's got his eyebrows pulled together, and there's a deep crease in his forehead. I reach for something to say, and notice, looking between the wide-spaced houses across the street and up the hill, that I can see into the backyard of a ruined, burnt house. Roof mostly gone, its scarred timbers reach up to the sky like naked arms above a deep green tangle of vines and gnarled trees.

"I suppose the neighborhood kids do have easier places to get in, for their fun." I comment.

Danny looks off somewhere across the street, maybe to the ruin I see through the yards, but behind his sunglasses I really can't tell exactly where it is he's looking.

At the foot of his mother's steps I turn to look up. This is a two-storey house with an attic, which still has *its* roof on, from the looks of things. It is built up on a field stone foundation so even the first floor is tall off the ground. There's a gracious front porch on the lower floor that currently looks like a sway backed donkey collapsing under vines. The whole thing is on a pretty big hill. It stands tall, the steep peak of the old gable roof making it look taller. Majestic even. Mysterious under the overgrown plants.

"How old is this house?"

"Built in the mid-twenties or so, I think. Ma and I moved here in the sixties and I lived here 'til I was ten."

"Oh," I'm trying to wrap my head around the years. I really want to know why and how Danny left home *at age ten*, but I don't want to pry. "I've a brother kinda your age. He was born in sixty-three."

"Me too, Miss Em!" Danny says, pleased. "I'm 1963

as well."

"Ha! Funny." I am trying not to say he looks older. "And it's just 'Em'."

My unasked question about what he did when he was ten hangs in the air for a moment. Maybe Danny doesn't notice it. I want to tell him about Will, who I call my brother but is actually my half-brother—but I don't. The words make my tongue start working mutely in my mouth, alive as I am in my sweaty adrenaline urge towards camaraderie, but I don't really know Danny. So my Will story hangs in the air too: the brother I love, and think about all the time but see rarely.

Will hasn't stayed at my house, our family's house, in years because the last time he stayed over he stole the tiny Japanese netsuke carvings off the mantel. They were small and only somewhat valuable—maybe worth two hundred dollars each—and there had been three of them. They were certainly precious to me, and now they were lost somewhere, sold somewhere, irretrievable. We had a big fight over the netsuke. I am still trying to repair the rift it caused between us. I have long since decided that I'd rather have Will steal my things than be out on the street alone. I'd rather see him more often, even if the price is missing tchotchkes from my mantel. Will still stops by sometimes to chat, sitting with me on the porch because he won't come in even if I offer. I always offer. These days I always hope he'll come in. He's more unpredictable than a startled squirrel. I never know where he's living. He can't keep hold of a cellphone for more than a couple of weeks, so I seldom have a number for him either.

I neither ask nor say any of the things I am actually thinking about. I press my tongue against the backs of my front teeth, still myself, take a breath, and then ask:

"You wanna start heading back?" I look down at Girlfriend. Carrying her will be nasty because she's hot and I'm already really sweaty and her fur will shed off on me and stick to my sweat. Plus, I don't why, but hound dogs just smell terrible in the sun. Must be something about their long lips, too much mucus membrane or something. Danny must see some look on my face as I contemplate the problem of my naughty little beagle bitch.

"Hang on . . . Em. I got something back here, I think. I used to anyway." He takes the cracked concrete steps two at a time and strides to the side of the porch using his arms to push aside thickly grown plants which include, I see now, lush and abundant poison ivy. He re-emerges seconds later with a coiled length of blue plastic kitchen string.

"Some of this hold her, you think?"

"Yeah! Thanks. Hey, you know you're *in* poison ivy, right?"

Danny laughs "It doesn't bother me. I'm lucky." He pulls a pocket knife from his pants pocket and cuts off a length of string, disappears under the porch again and comes back out with just the length he's cut off.

"How come you know where the string is if you haven't lived here since you were ten?"

"Ha!" Danny coughs "Well now that's a bit of a story."

He stops there, but I keep looking at him expectantly, so he adds "When Ma died, I packed her stuff up and gave it all away. Cleaned the place out."

He pauses, and I am still looking at him. He leans down as if to check his laces are still tied and says to his shoes with a tone of wrapping up, concluding, "It's useful to have some string and odds and ends out here so I don't have to go in and out of the house, get the boards off."

That sort of, but doesn't really answer my question. It's odd to me that Danny doesn't live in this house. It's close to where he is living up on Coldspring, and much nicer. It has shade trees, a front and probably a back yard. It must be pretty awful inside now after twenty years of no upkeep, but I bet it was comfy enough back when Danny was ten, even when he was eighteen I bet it was pretty OK in there. Maybe three bedrooms and a bath? I wonder what it is like now, behind the boarded-up windows and doors. I wonder how bad the disrepair is.

Danny saying he packed the place up makes me think of what had been in there when it was all furnished. What did he pack? For a moment I enjoy imagining that the place is untouched, the furniture and decorations all left exactly in place. I have a fleeting but vivid mental image of an orange sofa with a plastic cover on it, and a green shag rug. God, I hate shag. It makes me laugh to myself: a beautiful 1920s house with a ghastly 1970s living room. I wonder why my brain cooked *that* image up.

I take the blue string and tie it to Girlfriend's collar with an excessive tangle of knots. No way is she crossing York Road on her own this time; no way is she taking off again.

"Thanks, Danny. This'll work great."

"Good. Good. You go on ahead. I'm going to stay here a while."

I don't want to go on ahead if Danny's staying. I am nosy, curious about this beautiful wreck of a house, but he's ushered us off now, so I don't feel like I have the option of hanging around with him.

"Uhm, Ok. Thanks again." I go to shake his hand, and he uses the handshake to pull me in closer and give me a hug, patting my back as he does so, which reassures me there's no mistaken romantic interest here; it's just a friendly hug.

"Bye, Em. I'm glad you got your dog."

"Me too. And thanks again for all your help. I really appreciate it."

I tug reluctant Girlfriend to her feet and we cross Alhambra to start the slow walk up the hot steep hill of Radnor towards York Road. I turn to look back when I'm about half-way up, relieved to have the afternoon sun at my back and off my face for a moment, and look for Danny. He's standing in the overgrowth, looking up at the house from the side. He appears to be neck-deep in plants, in poison ivy I imagine. He's just standing there looking up. I can't see what he's looking at. The way he stands, the shape of him, height, and posture, all look like Will to me.

At first, there were trees, their roots gnarled in the iron-rich clay around heavy Coldspring gneiss. There was a stream in the bottom of a valley. Tall oak, chestnut, and hickory whispered in the breeze of slow time, sylvan historians. In the night airs, there were maelstroms of great green luna moths, wings like downy leaves with eyes painted upon them.

Then the rivers were forced underground, and secrets were hidden along with beauty. Acorns, each a story in a nutshell, were hidden high in the branches, up in the trees, up high.

Danny

Linnie fell and it was my fault.

It had been such a hot day already. The curtains were drawn to keep the mid-afternoon sun out, but they made the air heavy, more like something solid that was holding you down. The sweat ran to my bellybutton, my hair was a hot, wet sponge on my head, and my legs felt like they were bloated sweaty brown hotdogs not skinny skateboard-riding legs. The air was heavy as a sweaty diaper. It smelled like a diaper too, because baby Linneah was dirty, there weren't any disposables left, and the cloth diapers in the basket smelled moldy. So I wasn't changing her. It smelled and it made her cry in her crib. She yelled and lay on her back wiggling her arms trying to roll over.

Ma had gone up to work in Towson. It wasn't on her usual schedule, and this time Linnie and I couldn't come because it was too messy there, she said. Us kids'd have to stay home alone, Ma said, just for a few hours, and I could be a big boy because seven is almost a man and I'd have to look after us both.

Someone had broken into the Legion hall that Ma cleaned and catered for. They had smashed a window, turned the party tables upside down and done something else she wouldn't tell us. "On the *wall*?" she had gasped into the phone when the call came. "Oh my Lord, those protesters have gone too far this time."

People were protesting the war in Vietnam. That much I knew. Some man from Govans even went to the White House in Washington DC with his little baby girl. He set himself on fire, right there, in front of her, to protest. I wonder whatever happened to her, that baby, after watching her daddy die like that. Some people hated the war so much. They hated soldiers like my Daddy who had died there when I was only two, and even pilots like Ma's new husband John who was Linnie's Daddy.

Ma fell in love with John at a dance at the Legion hall. He had loved the donuts she made. She had loved his tall thin body and air force uniform. She loved his big hands.

I didn't love John then or ever.

Ma had loved my daddy first she said, but they were young. Ma named me Daniel, Danny for short, because of the lion's den story in the Bible and how my being born into her family when she was just an unmarried girl was like my being born into a den of angry lions. They were sixteen when I was born, and Daddy died when he was eighteen. I don't remember him at all. He enlisted as soon as he could and was dead after only ten days in combat. Ma says that's why she works at the Legion, to be closer to the memory of people like my daddy. Back then, I wished John would die too, or that he'd stay at the war and somehow, magically, my daddy would come home instead. But John's plane always kept him above the bullets.

The sweltering air in the house made my head foggy, achy. Linnie was screaming and screaming in her crib and it was so hot. My head was hurting and I just wanted to lie on the couch. It had been too hot for lunch, but I had drunk some of the strawberry kool-aid Ma left in the jug for me. Linnie had not wanted to take her bottle. The formula looked lumpy. Maybe Ma hadn't mixed it very well as she was rushing to leave. Poor Linnie was dirty and hungry. We were both hot. I took pity on her. I thought I'd better at least try to change her.

I got Linnie and put her on the change-table. I started to go to the kitchen to find the hamper with the cloth diapers, but walked past the couch on the way. I felt heavier and more tired with each humid step. The couch looked cool and inviting. I couldn't help it. I lay down. I flopped down on my front, face into the cushion, legs sticky on the plastic cover. Linnie's screaming was so constant I covered my ears with my palms and pressed hard.

Then it was quiet. I took my hands away from my head. Delicious, wonderful quiet that made the air seem darker and cooler.

Then panic, then guilt, hand in hand like Jack and Jill heading up the hill. I jumped off the couch, turned to the change-table. Linnie had fallen. She had rolled and fallen. I saw her body head down, one of her fat brown legs tangled with the blond wood of the change table's leg and one hooked by the back of her knee onto the white lower shelf. Linnie's face was away from me, crushed into the green of the carpet. I couldn't touch her at first. I just stood there on tip toe trying to breathe but the breaths wouldn't come anything other than tiny and fast. It took me a few minutes. Finally I did lift her, roll her, feel her soft slackness. I laid her flat on the floor and stared. She came to, startling me, her eyes wide and brown, breaths wet and short, but she didn't cry.

From Below

See them, how they grow, their short lives, the people clustered around them: petals and sepals on a stem.

See the thin man aching around the cold at his core. See the dog walker, still on the lip of my rolling landscape where she tries to make sense of how it all goes together.

From here, the past and future everywhen themselves, they overlap: adult baby child.

See its sameness: just one humantime.

The dogwalker and the thin man.

See a constellation, the electric-bright points clear as you see up through the grasses.

Connect the brights to see the whole, the spangle, the interconnection.

Time is long for me, and short for them. Their lives rush past, the space between the wetness of their birth and the dryness of their dying. Still, I feel them long enough to know that they are of me.

It is harder now. They do not reach for me the way they used to. It used to be true that some loved me. They would see a shape in a plant, tree, hill or valley that made them feel at peace, or they would place a palm flat to my soil, put a naked foot in a cold river on a slippery stone. They wanted me, needed me, knew how we were part of the same long story.

Now it is hard to know what they love, or how. I have fallen into invisibility behind the glass windows of their cars and houses. I hold them every day, yet they do not see me. More of them are closed into themselves these days too, in an unhappiness turned inward. Their eyes roll in to taunt their souls. They try, even in the short breath of their lives, to smother the feeling of being themselves.

I see the most lost of them lean down as if towards me, but they are falling, miserably intoxicated, into a tormented vision of themselves. I cannot help these people. I want to catch them and love them up from their stupor, putting the wonder of existing into them, but they do not see me, do not reach for me, and I cannot touch them, even when they fall.

The thin man I want to still into calm. He was a boy when his sister fell down and then died young: his unease has bitten deep into his flesh. This one I can tend because he reaches for me, for the house on my soil, for the roots in the earth that make him and ground him here. The woman, the dog walker, she reaches beyond the human construction to my contours and tries to find meaning. She tries to know me.

A dream, in and out of their time, these I can give to the thin man and the dogwalker.

My gift will be their knowing they have been in the right place.

Well, this isn't what I thought I was going to be doing today. I had no plans to come to Ma's house. I thought I'd have a nice afternoon hanging out with Tyrell, drink some iced tea, play some gin rummy maybe, and then settle down to do the books for "Here to Home: Send Money Anywhere in the World." They have a small bungalow on York Road covered with a mural of African grasslands done before Baltimore murals became a trendy thing. Their spreadsheets are always a mess. Money going to Lomé, Juba and Port-au-Prince. All kinds of places. Usually export in USD, but sometimes in the local currency or Euros. Complicated books. I always do the numbers for these guys quarterly so that come tax time things aren't too bad to make sense of. Habib, the owner, pays me under the table, and he always tips too.

I was actually kind of looking forward to doing the work. I'd turn on the a/c unit in my kitchen in back and sit at my unfashionable Dell Latitude 3350 laptop (who needs a Mac anyway?) right in front of it, letting the cold wind make my ear drums hurt. I like focusing on the numbers and puzzling out how the exchange rates and wire transfer fees all work into the bottom line.

Thinking about "Here to Home" reminds me that I have another prospect I want to check out: the new tag and title place. It's in the tall white stone building up near the Popeye's and the post office. I've heard the white building was the home of a senator once, a senator who was the father of a famous silent movie starlet. Place must've been huge for a single family. It's been remodeled into separate spaces now, and, according to the sign out front, has a bunch of clinics, counsellors, and social workers. That all makes sense because these folks must get a lot of their business from the Glenwood Center just along York Road. Glenwood helps the addicts, and refers them over up here for additional kinds of help, or vice-versa.

Anyway, the tag and title place is new and their little strip of poster on the billboard outside the building has, buried at the bottom of its blurb, the enticing claim that they do "Auto Export to Africa." Sounds like these guys could use some of my international accounting expertise, right? And I could do, I could always do, with being reminded that there's a rest of the world out there that carries on existing even though I only exist here now, only in this place not all the other possible ones, and not in any of the ones I dream of returning to or living in.

Any international work is gravy, and it's all better work than the boredom of tax time. Occasionally there'll be some real crooked stuff in the tax work people give me. That's kind of fun, like gossip. My job then is to conceal illegal things as best I can. Mostly though, I find out how little money people actually have and how they are bouncing credit card debt off bank loans on their way to bankruptcy or petty crime.

Anyway, I am not at home now. I am in Ma's yard.

The garden is a mess. I should come by with a weed whacker and some garden shears and beat the plants back before I get a ticket from the city. I told that woman with the dogs, Em, that I don't get squatters. I hope that's true. I never have before, but I actually haven't checked for a while. It certainly doesn't look like anyone's come through the bushes recently. And there's no smell. If someone was living here, they'd have to shit somewhere. Water and electric have been off for twenty years, so there'd be a smell. Squirrels worry me more than people, as do rats and raccoons. I cleared the house out mostly after Ma died, but there's still the attic to worry about. I don't want rodents digging into things up there.

The plants are so overgrown that it's hard to walk around the house. The boards on the front door, porch doors and on the downstairs windows are still good. Back door is still boarded up too. The wooden steps up to the back door have come away from the house: they look like a row boat that shipwrecked on poison ivy.

I come around the side to where you can look up and see the bathroom window upstairs. It's a pretty thing, and unusual too. On top there's a half circle of green and blue stained glass made to look like a peacock. Under the peacock is a rectangular casement window. I stand for a while and look up at it. The tree near the house there has nasty carpet moths and there're webs from its nearest branch spun out to the window and the side of the house. Spider webs up there too, from the looks of it. The window itself is dark because of the shade from the trees and the unlit room behind it. I wonder if the bathroom door is closed in there? Did I leave it closed? The yard used to be brighter on this side of the house, before the trees grew so big. I see in my head how the bathroom floor with its little black and white tiles would look green and blue when the light shone through. The colors in my mind come along with the sound of water dripping in the white enamel bathtub with the red rust stain under the faucet.

Something bites me on the back of my neck, fly or mosquito, and I slap at the spot. It shakes me out of my memories. Time to go back up to my Coldspring home. But not quite yet. I'd like to give Em a bit more time to get her dog up the street. I don't want to walk with her. I like her. She seems like a nice person, always ready to give me a big smile. But I don't want to talk to her about the house. I can't believe her dog ran down here like that. It came right here and sat right on these steps.

We never had a dog here when I was a boy, though I wanted one, just like most other little boys want a dog. Ma was always scared of them, and claimed they made too much mess. John liked them well enough but he was hardly ever here, so his vote didn't count. No pets here. But there was that little dog on the steps like it was her house she'd come home to. It should be funny to me, a coincidence to joke about with Tyrell if I see him later, but instead it's an uneasy feeling I have, one I don't want to talk about. Tyrell knows I don't like to talk about the house.

I can tell Tyrell almost anything these days. We've been neighbors and lazy old geezers on my porch since when my Ma was still alive, the whole time I was divorcing Allidah and we were fighting about every little damn thing. I've listened to him talk about his kids and their troubles (a son in prison, a son killed, a daughter who had a rough patch and gave him grandkids way too early but now has a job as a medical technician at a urology office and a fierce commitment to her church). He knows most of my troubles too, with marriage and infidelity and the nastiness of a bad divorce. He also knows well enough that the Alhambra house, Ma's house, is a sore spot for me, that I definitely don't want advice about the property market or selling the thing. He knows I don't like to talk about the house.

EM

When I lived in Ednor Gardens, I used to walk on my own every morning: I didn't have the dogs yet, but I guess I've always been an aspiring dog walker. I'd cut through the side streets and cross York over into Guilford, where even the row houses are huge, the sidewalks wide and well-maintained, the gardens lush with hydrangeas and clematis over arched decorative gateways. There was less traffic in Guilford, and more greenery. It felt like there was better air to breathe. I'd jay walk across York with its abundant curb-garbage, go through the pedestrian arch in the wall that kept Guilford and York Road separate, and then be in a leafy quietness.

I had favorite routes: past the house with all the mint (the mint walk), past the house with tree stumps covered in fungi (the mushroom walk) and my favorite, past the house with at least seventeen cats (the cat walk). If I timed the cat walk right, I'd see Eleanor, the elderly woman who raised the ire of her neighbors by feeding all of those cats tinned wet food off paper plates on her front steps every morning at eight. From any of these routes, I'd usually choose to come back along 39th Avenue. I'd cross York at the light and then cut through a different set of side streets as I headed south east, and home.

It was on the return that I usually passed through the malodorous shattered-glass and litter filled alley which

I thought of as "Rat Alley" because I almost always saw rats there. Urban and unperturbed by the proximity of humans, these rats were fat and placid, with glossy brown pelts. They'd scamper along in pairs or triplets, genial-looking, except for their alarming hairless tails and sinister yellow incisors.

Rat Alley ended in front of "Tony's, A Nice Quiet Place to Drink." I never drank there for two reasons: one, by then I was trying to be pretty much teetotal, and two because in spite of its name, it looked like a good rowdy place to get stabbed. The row houses along the alley had tiny, generally filthy, dark, and rat-infested yards, though sometimes their fences were graced with a beautiful purple morning glory, growing abundant and gorgeous in spite of being considered a weed. I'd see Girlfriend wagging behind the chain link of one of those yards when I was still a long way off. She'd see me and start wagging, her whole body arcing side to side. She'd let out her hound voice and howl and howl for me. I'd call back:

"Hey, Girlfriend! How ya' doin'?"

I'd get to her, lean over the fence and scratch her filthy back, making my fingers dark grey and tacky. We'd talk, her and me, about her distended nipples. How many puppies had she had? And about how cute she was in spite of being so skinny, so dirty. She had a filthy doghouse in that tiny yard with no grass and she lived out there all summer, as well as all winter.

When I knew I was going to move back to Kernewood, to Kerneway Avenue, back to the 1950 fieldstone house that had been my childhood home, I decided to steal Girlfriend. I just showed up one day with a collar and a leash, walked down the alley as usual, and took her. There was a tense moment when the gate wouldn't open and I realized I'd have to climb in to get her and lift her out with me, but really the fence was only three feet and the beagle less than thirty pounds so that was pretty easy. I'm glad I didn't get caught in the act. Girlfriend wasn't in great shape for running after so much time in a small yard, so we just walked away together, her tangling me with the leash, and startling at every unfamiliar thing (which was everything).

I only got Blue last fall, through my friend Bev who fosters animals for the Maryland SPCA. Dogs that are too sick or scared to go into the shelter come to her for a bit of rehabilitation before they are put up for adoption. Blue had been transferred here from a "kill" shelter in Virginia where he'd spent five weeks not eating. I guess the cages and close proximity of other dogs stressed him out. He'd gotten thin. The MDSPCA wanted him, probably because they are always looking for something other than pit bulls with massive heads like cinder blocks to offer the general adopting public. I met Blue when Bev had a couple of people over on a Friday evening for drinks and grilled chicken. He was curled up in the corner between the back of her couch, the patio doors and the wall. He had long white legs freckled brown, a brown skinny body, a narrow chestnut head with eyelids drooping around his big round eyes, and bloodhound ears and lips. He was clearly a mixed breed hound, but a tall one.

I saw him and acted like I was ignoring him, because he looked like he was stressed and trying to hide and I didn't want to make him feel worse. On the patio, I sat with my back to the glass sliding door so my back was to him as well. Dogs like that. They know you aren't planning to do anything to them. I just sat; I didn't mill around (I am not great at party conversation anyway). After about a half hour, he'd crept outside and was behind my chair. I put my hand out and he came forward to touch it with his nose, and then he let me reach under his chin and scratch it. It felt like a little handshake, a moment of complicity. I wanted him. There was an adoption process, and I had to wait a while till he was officially out of foster care but then he came to live with me and Girlfriend.

So now I don't just have one dog who wasn't socialized properly as a puppy, but two. Other dog walkers avoid me because my guys set up a howling-shrieking-spinning-in-circles hackles-raised racket if they see another animal. Nonetheless, I walk the dogs every morning, as early as I can, and every afternoon before five, to try and minimize encounters with other dog walkers. We have our Kernewood routes: Loyola (up the hill to the memorial circle at Notre Dame with it's pretty view), Whiteford (which involves following the alley or "lane" to Winston and then up Whiteford onto Notre Dame lane and back down Norwood), the Tulip garden (around Sherwood gardens in Guilford; you have to be up really early for that to work out—lots of people with dogs over there), the candy-cane walk (past the house that does crazy Christmas decorations) and now a new one on the other side of York: Alhambra Avenue, past Danny's mother's house.

Danny is standing, watching the river of traffic flow past, sun warming the ground.

He thinks about how this strip of street is so different from the neighborhoods behind him. Sun on him, he faces a hot rush of exhaust, while behind his house there are shade trees, as well as a row of garages with the roofs collapsing, full of dead cars and live rats. At the other end of the alley, there are yards with blooming flowers and trees. *Another neighborhood*, he thinks, like there is some dividing line. Across Coldspring, a few blocks over to the west there's Sherwood Gardens, planted thick with tulips, ringed by mansions. *Another world*, he thinks. All that money, those houses with all their bedrooms and chandeliers, those Dutch flowers foreign in the soil and fed and watered more abundantly than the urchins shrieking on his neighbor's stoop.

But it is all one place.

Em is walking her dogs again, big and small. Danny can see their shadows stretching out behind them. She's a strange foreshortened Kalahari bush ghost, flanked by skinny slavering hyenas: the shadows lurch, lumpy, and uneven.

Afternoon sun, shimmering with heat. He imagines the shadows peeling off on their own to run *hiyiyiyiyah!* down the alley away.

Danny's Ma's house is in a deep valley, surrounded by other old houses, some in OK shape, some total wrecks, many on surprisingly big plots of land. For just a square half-mile or so, it feels rural over there, like a sleepy piece of old countryside. The overgrown lots, with their big-knuckled oak trees, ancient dead braches lying where they fall, shrouded in thick vines, make the air taste better than up on York Road and make it easier to imagine this spot as a pastoral landscape. I am struck by the curve of the hills, their gracious sweep. I try to see the place through a squint, to imagine it all as one, to see the row houses and streaming traffic as trees and rivers. Then I am surprised by how expansive the place seems, like one wide swath of land that was once lovely.

It's a longer route for me, so I save it for Sunday mornings when I have more time. There's less traffic on Sunday mornings at six too, so I can jay walk across York with impunity, which is eerie. York Road *without* traffic is a magical, unusual thing. The Alhambra route also sets me walking east across York into the dawn, when the sky is pink and the clouds pearly. The sky is so lovely then, a cliché prettiness. The gas station, dentist office and Gomez Tires are purely ugly, but in the dawn light, and with the quiet street, you can almost forget.

It has been several Sundays now that I have walked

past the boarded up house on Alhambra, as slowly as I can. In the mornings it is shady down there, the overgrowth of plants dark and lush. I want to go up to the house, to go in. I probably would try if there wasn't so much poison ivy, and if my dogs were better at being subtle; they aren't subtle. They are heavy-footed, loud and unpredictable. They do, however, give me a reason to be out walking, and lately, lurking, on Alhambra on Sunday mornings. At that hour I only run into the earliest of Church-goers, and it's nice to at least seem to have a reason to be walking past their houses. Sometimes I go down the alley behind Danny's Ma's house, so I've seen its backyard (also overgrown) and the steps that have fallen off the back of the house. The downstairs windows are all boarded up, the plywood grey and warping with age. Upstairs they aren't, but you'd need a tall ladder to get up there, and on the slope it would be difficult to do it safely.

I am starting to feel self-conscious when I see Danny on the afternoon dogwalk around the block, the short route that always goes past his house. Do I need to tell him I'm stalking his mother's house? Maybe not. I do want to ask him about it though. I want to find out more. We always chat a bit, him on his porch, me on the sidewalk, yelling over the noise of the traffic. We never talk about anything real, just the weather, the dogs. How does one get from there to asking questions about someone's actual life? I am in my forties and I have friends, so I must have made this leap before. But now I can't remember how to do it effortlessly, which means that pretty much every afternoon after chatting meaninglessly with Danny I think hard—effortfully—about how to befriend him.

Often Danny's friend Tyrell, with his caved-in face like someone who probably has no molars behind his cheeks, is out there on the sweltering sunny porch too.

I don't know why they don't sit somewhere shady and cool. It's always a relief to walk off Coldspring into the shade of Kerneway. It feels like a different, quieter, world once I've made that turn.

Back-yard beetle, black in the iron-red soil under the dry grass of the heat. Narrow of abdomen, wings faintly ridged, thorax tipped prominently with two strong ebony-dark thorns. Clicks through the dryness, finds an aphid, translucent in the sun, resting on a clover flower. Hungry swift click grab.

My soil is dry but loose, dusty in the grass-filtered sun.

Naked soil.

Far from here, wind and flood have washed concrete and tarmac into disarray in order that the strong green weeds may grow through, the beetles and ants find their way.

Far from here, earthquake: the soil cleaves, tumbles, feels the relief of air and sun.

Someday the shoreline will rise up and this hill will smell the brackish salt of ocean.

A dog's turd stinks in the heat. Two hornets, smooth in their yellow-black armor, rest in its odor, waiting for the iridescent blue-green buzz of flies it will attract. They hear the beetle before they see it, watch it grab aphid and clover petal. Watch the beetle scratch back into my dry soil.

Summer.

The pleasure of the small piece of naked earth: no concrete, no tarmac, no buildings or roads.

This yard feels small. Chain-link fence and an iron gate as if the trees would run away.

Sometimes the hot days in Baltimore smell like Ghana, maybe most forcefully so when one is in an air-conditioned space and then opens a door and the humid air rushes to meet you. Where hot/cold, wet/dry collide, it smells like coming out of a rare and wonderful air conditioned room in Ghana.

Nothing smells like Buduburam though.

I grew up on Kerneway, and when I finally left I went *just* out of state to Dickinson College. Then, the experience that was supposed to be definitive, transformative, the one that was supposed to clarify who I was going to be as an adult and change me into someone more interesting and vital: I went to Ghana for two years with the Peace Corps to dig wells for Liberian and Sierra Leonean refugees at Buduburam camp, in Accra.

The refugee camp was pungent with banana peel, palm oil, and sweat, but reeked too of despair and frustration. Refugees came from Liberia, daily. When I was there, the camp was expanding so much and so quickly that the best the aid workers could offer was squalor. Safety, perhaps, but not much else. Basic shelter and potable water were urgent priorities. Sewage needed places to go so that it wouldn't get washed out and flow through the muddy tents when the rain hammered down like a Biblical apocalypse. Liberian kids needed balls to play soccer with, and school to go to. I was hot, and bloated. I watched the thin, fast kids playing soccer incredulously: how could they move in the heat? Some of them had open sores on their legs from guinea worm, and even those kids were more active than I was.

The aid workers got together on the weekends sometimes, and carpooled in one of the white Isuzu Troopers to nearby Kokrobitey for access to the beach, and drinks and entertainment at AAMAL (The Academy of African Music and Arts). We'd sit in the beach sand, or swim cautiously, mindful of the spiky sea urchins clinging to the rocks under the turbulent water. Then we'd come up to AAMAL and sit on their white wooden beach chairs and watch a kente-bright drum and dance performance while drinking cold Star beer.

One of those weekends, I got roped into a dance class. I learned the female part of the *swanti,* "swan tease," along with an elderly and determined German tourist, while two of the drummers left their Djembes and played the male dance parts. The choreography involved shuffling in a circle, always in a slight crouch, torso tipped forwards, butt stuck out behind. My thighs burned. Afterwards I took a shower in the outdoor shower stall, enjoying the cold water gushing freely out of a pipe onto my head, my skin naked to the sky. The next day my legs were so stiff that I could only get into the Isuzu by using my left hand on the roof of the vehicle and then lowering with that arm's strength, not using my legs at all.

A stint in Ghana was what it took to sweat the child out of me. There, I was always hungry but gained weight drinking too much bottled coca-cola and fanta because even the water from the wells I helped dig wasn't potable to a delicate western constitution. The refugees could drink the water; the expat aid workers would get really sick from it. Instead of inspiring me on to great things, Buduburam bloated and dead-ended me. It made it clear that I didn't want to go into international aid. I didn't know what I wanted to do instead.

I came back, and lived with strangers in a shared mansion in Bolton Hill for a few years, and worked at three different restaurants washing dishes. I spent my meager dishwashing dollars every night at the Mount Royal Tavern with the colorful Maryland Institute College of Art and Design students, the tougher regulars, and the young bucks who'd head out to wrestle on the grass median in the midst of traffic every night once they were drunk enough.

Every night I too drank. I got meaner and poorer. One night I mugged a girl just because she was an art school student so cute and flush with cash it made me angry. I hit on her at the bar, complimented her on her carefully ripped grungy jeans, and big plastic hoop earrings. Not too much later we stumbled out into the alley behind the bar and made out, with her back to the concrete wall and me pressed up against her. You could count on a MICA girl to want to kiss another girl once in a while. It was one identity-shifting adventure among so many others that make up the social culture of college. Then I stepped back, grabbed her shoulders and shoved this small girl hard into the wall so that the air huffed out of her. I jammed the back of my elbow hard into the notch where her thin soft throat dipped between her collar bones. Her eyes went wide with surprise and she couldn't yell because she was still winded from the shove. I slapped the side of her head as hard as I could with my free hand, slipped her Hello Kitty wallet out of her back jeans pocket, and let her fall so she could double over and choke on her own soreness. I took her money, dropped the wallet on the ground and walked away. I'm lucky she didn't call the police on me. Later that night I sat in my room and wept over what a jerk I had become and how I didn't know what to do or where to go in the world. I stopped going to the tavern.

I wonder why I am still in Baltimore, and why I couldn't get away. I went to Dickinson which should have left me full of ambition and potential and then I went all the way to Ghana. How much further do you need to go? What else do you need to become successful, determined, to have a real career, to grow up, to move away? But I came back, all the way back, back to my very own childhood home like somehow this was the bottom of a valley and I was a pebble that kept rolling back to its starting point no matter how hard you flung it up the hill.

Long past, when I was green, the estates of wealthy men tamed the plants and let the hills show from under the trees they razed to make more picturesque the deep valley where the river once wanted to run, and a man named Walters built an ornamental lake.

Their houses were made of so-called random stone pulled from my heart, and wood from the land itself. My land was plotted and fenced, but you could see how it rolled and swooped.

The Indian trail, like an arrow shot north, ran along the flattest ridge of my spine.

I missed the trees, pines, oaks, tulip poplars, and chestnuts when they took so many down, chewing out the stumps with their metal tools. The stumps clung in so hard.

There were once horse drawn trams, trains, and double-deck horse cars. Paving the road, York Road, route 45 they call it, came later, as did the streetcar on its tracks. The two big greenhouses came and grew full of flowers, roses, carnations and white lilies, that were not like the chicory and dandelion that brightened my hills.

With the pavement, and the greenhouses, came a pollen-dispersal of houses, some standing free in a patch of sun and grass with a new wye oak, or two pretty willows planted to offer shade.

Houses with gabled roofs over their windows like human faces: windows like eyes and roofs like raised eyebrows, perpetually asking.

Worst of all were the houses in rows. Like endless molars in a convoluted jaw they erupted; rows and rows of teeth biting my swoops and curves into angles and pieces. By the time the cars came, they were all over me. A never-ending maw of row houses eating up my beauty, all conjoined. No eyes, just teeth.

Seasons went and there were fires in the city, arguments between the humans over the ill-treatment of those who had nothing by those who believed it just that they owned everything. The people became fewer, and then some of the houses stood empty. Some people moved away with big cars and long trucks full of fine furniture that still smelt dimly of my forests.

Eventually, other people came, on the bus, or by motorcycle, or in small cars, with plastic things that smelt like nowhere, and they started to fall down. These new people were unsure how to belong to me. They did not want to belong to me.

Some wanted to belong to another place, far away, a different continent, lost across a sea-passage.

Some could maybe be made to feel they wanted to belong here, but only if all my houses and roads could be remade to reflect their comforts back at them, not the abandoned legacies of paler, wealthier folk who took too much. These newer residents wanted my human history to be different, and because the marks of human history, buildings and roads, were awful to them, they could not see me.

Unsure of how, or if, they could stand up in this place and be one with me, many cultivated a habit of ignoring me altogether. Instead of planting flowers or trees, they laid plastic grass and concrete upon the soil.

Blanketed, hidden, I cannot reach to them; they feel me unhomely still. They treat me badly, leaning out of their cars to throw bags, bottles, cans and boxes down, making me ugly in spite of my rolling hills and ancient river valleys.

Long and wide as I see it, this moment's sadnesses will not persist.

I can and do in their small time, small things.

But across the slow time as seasons speed and vast plates of earth below grumble, the humans will all be gone: this dusty concrete gasoline tumult, hot and asphyxiating, will be still and calm.

All these bones will be compressed under the weight of immense trees that have not yet even sprouted from acorns, under the dust of volcanoes that have not yet pushed peaks up from beneath, under the waters that will rise and shift.

Em

My grandfather liked to brag that his son, my father, had bought this house on Kerneway "brand new!" Grandpa remembered the neighborhood from earlier, from his childhood in Baltimore during the first war, and the years just after.

"My son bought one of the first houses on old Mr. Wilson's estate!" he'd holler deafly.

"I remember Wilson's own house just up the avenue. Me and my brother used to come here to pick mulberries in the woods and to throw rocks at his pair of cranky old donkeys. We'd be on our way to buy candy from Snyder's up on York Road. Oh those two old Snyder ladies sure knew how to make tasty sweet goodies, and we'd cut through Wilson's land." Licking his lips, and laughing. The scant hair on his chin trembled with pleasure recollecting the taste and vicious joy of those young "rambles" along York road.

Grandpa remembered wrong. Dad's house wasn't part of the first development on Wilson's land. When I did some research on the old Wilson estate, it turned out Wilson had sold a parcel of land in 1910, and that had been developed into tidy row houses all along what was called Kernwood Road. Kerneway Avenue, where my father's fieldstone house was built in 1950, actually followed the arc of Wilson's old driveway.

I guess Dad did buy the house new, but it wasn't even the first house on *that* road. There were others built earlier, in the forties. Some of those were brick. Maybe there had been cranky donkeys when Grandpa was a child, but even that seems questionable. When Dad bought the house he was single, but already making good money as a dentist. My mother came to work for him as a hygienist a little more than a decade later. She didn't move into this house til the mid-sixties, after he'd been there for fifteen years, making it a tidy but unornamented bachelor pad. Her big project, which the two of them saved up for, was the drastic redecoration which happened in 1973, when I was only three, and which I thankfully do not remember.

Grandpa was prone to exaggeration in pursuit of a good story, which was great for Will and me when we'd visit him. The stories always involved props, like candy he'd carefully pull from a drawer with his arthritic fingers. "Not as good as the Snyder sisters's, but can you two check if it's tasty?" Or ice cream taken from the freezer which he'd claim was made from the milk of Wilson's own donkeys. "Donkeys don't give milk" my father would school us, sternly, before glaring at his father to stop filling our heads with nonsense.

Grandpa's embroidered truths made my father a sour and taciturn truth-teller, when he wasn't indulging in the anodyne of alcohol (sadly Johnny Walker Black Label did nothing to relieve him from silent resentment or, violent outbursts).

My father's drinking was an equal to my garrulous mother's *Valley of the Dolls*-style reliance on pills. Mother was full of creative energy. She could paint, throw pots, do macramé and made even copper enamel work look easy. She could be cheerful and sprightly. It made sense that her name, Bridget, became "Birdie" to everyone who knew her. My father, Brian, was always simply Brian. Birdie was buxom, gregarious, and flamboyant, with curly red Germanic hair, pale skin, freckles, and as the years went by, a serious dependence on valium by the handful. Unsurprising, the valium, for even as children Will and I noticed that her hands, when she wasn't watching them, opened and clenched nervously, continuously, like she was grabbing onto something and then crushing it. Perhaps she was grasping and crushing her guilt about her choice to leave her first husband (Will's father), for her boss (mine).

Will and I loved the rumpus room, not a room really, but an area at the back of the house next to the kitchen which had a couch, a small TV with a large antenna, and a coffee table where we were allowed to leave our toys and games. There was a larger area adjoining the other side of the kitchen where my mother had put the dining table. At the front of the house was a marble-floored entry way with a tall, imposing section of fieldstone wall blocking the view to a big living room and its gas fireplace. Except the kitchen, the whole downstairs had blue shag carpets (courtesy of Mother's 1973 remodel). The shag was pretty much the only thing I was intent on removing before I moved back in as an adult. Turned out there was pale pine underneath the old carpet, so now I have wood floors.

When I was small, Will and I played with my Fisher Price toys in the rumpus room. Will was seven years older, but he'd indulge me. He'd helped me give the bright little plastic characters names. George and Martha went on adventures in their VW van to places with atoms and positive or negative ions, which must have been what he was learning about at school. Or we'd play with Legos, trying to build "invincible bricks" that could be hurled from the sofa down onto the shag; the winning brick would be the one that used the most pieces but disintegrated least on impact. Will was the perfect brother all the way up until he became fifteen, handsome, and reckless, which is also when he discovered heroin.

At fifteen, he started to hang out with different kinds of friends, nastier friends, some older than him, one with a tattoo of a handgun on the hairless skin along the inside of his forearm. He'd bring these people home in the afternoons after school when Mom and Dad were still at work. At first I wanted to hang out with them and would sit in the corner of the rumpus room trying to be part of their weirdly boisterous conversations. Will was different when the others were there, rude and prone to a high whinnying laugh I never heard him use any other time. He never teased me, but the other boys did. Tall, chubby Mike Talermo made me cry by asking me repeatedly "what's a snatch?" and then laughing when I looked confused because clearly "snatch" to him meant something different than the "grab" action I knew it as.

Mike Talermo, big and loud with small brown eyes deep set in his piggy cheeks, swaggered into the bathroom once when I was in there, catching me on the toilet with my skirt up at my waist and my pale yellow panties around my ankles, my naked feet dangling just above the horseshoe-shaped orange shag rug that hugged the base of the toilet. I was eight, and small for my age.

"*Yo!*" he whispered managing to make the single word sound menacing as he stepped into the small room and closed the door behind him.

"*Yo,* you don't mind if I come in do you?"

I was scared. I shook my head No though I really did mind.

He sat on the rim of the bath, right next to me, and put his wide index finger between my legs, rubbing it back and forth on my hairless little girl pubis, on my tiny dry and terrified clitoris.

"Here's your *snatch*," he whispered and then he got up and walked out, leaving the bathroom door wide open behind him.

The dogwalker and the thin man: histories on different sides of York Road.

East and West. Black and White.

In this place they weave, bleed into the soil of each other, and of all who live, have lived, will live here. Lives seemingly separate and parallel are part of one story. The same lines in the earth over and over: individual histories commingled become one dream.

This long York Road of mine is a mirror and a seam, a join, a boundary that connects.

I, the liminal earth, the zone of connection not division. I hold their two lives, their two families, their memories, guilt, and new growth on this line, this place of journey and transition.

I wait for them to recognize each other in the mirror between their past and their future.

Sweet now. Gentle now.

Give them time to understand it, like a reflection

coming clearer on a windblown lake as the waters
gradually still.

Give them time to feel the earth under them.

Will, white-blond, thin arms scarred with eczema, is watching her scream. She's little—born underweight, premature, and still trying to catch up—but so angry. Her face is wrinkled like a balled-up Kleenex, scarlet, wet with tears. She's so mad her little fists are clenched and press down into the change table, helping her arch her back up as she presses her head and heels down; he can see a slim bright line of daylight under her body. At seven, he thinks he's old enough to change this diaper. Mother is in her leather recliner in the living room, with a headache. The snow is deep outside and the wind has brought the temperature so far below freezing that there's no going out today at all. You can feel the dryness in the air in your nose, where the skin tightens inside and pulls a bit with each breath. In the rumpus room you can feel the cold come from the wall. The plastic cover on top of the change table is cold to the touch.

First he got Mother the pills from the upstairs bathroom cabinet. "A handful of the pink ones" is what she always asked for. Now he is going to change the baby, this little pup, his sister. Really his half-sister. Given how much he hates this baby's dad, the man he never wanted to take his mother's time and attention, the man he had never wanted to live with, he's always surprised at how much he loves the baby. Her little wet puppy face. He kisses her angry forehead, having to lift slightly on his toes to get high enough above the table to bend over her.

Will turns to get a clean diaper and the butt cream that smells like playdough off of the dresser. Here too he has to stand slightly on tip toe to see. He's only got his back to her for a second, but that's long enough for little Em to roll. He turns, sees her falling, reaches out to catch, but merely touches her yellow footie-PJs as she falls, the penaten cream and diaper that he's dropped from his hands falling too. When she lands, he snatches her up instantly, as if he can erase the fall altogether if he's quick enough. It was so fast, and she's in his arms now. Maybe it didn't happen. It couldn't have happened. Nonetheless, in his eyes there's a flash photo image of her head bumping the blue shaggy floor. He keeps seeing it.

Holding her too tight and rocking: "It's OK, Emmie. It's OK. You're OK. You're OK."

Comforting himself more than her.

He pauses, looks into her little face: still crimson, wrinkled and screaming even harder now. But she's breathing. She's OK. She's crying. She's even angrier. Her little grey eyes glare at him.

He starts to cry too. Glad she's still there, still herself in those furious crying eyes.

Later she'll have a blue bump on her forehead, purple at its very center, and a smear of carpet burn on her cheek, and Will will look at the injuries and feel mostly relieved that she didn't die or bang her head into some kind of brain damage.

Hidden

Two squirrels argue over territory, over the right to
a tree. They flick their tails, thickly bearded heads of
wheat abruptly twitching tall over their backs. Up on a
high branch they wrestle, fall all the way to my earth,
heavy noisy tangle through plants as they tumble down.
They land hard, one on his back, the other managing
to come to the soft pads of his paws. The stronger, who
landed upright, chases the other who swerves through
vines and shadows. Zig-zag through the underbrush: to
a human this would look like a game of tag, but to the
squirrels it is an important struggle over nesting spaces
up high.

Pause: both chitter. A face off.

Then the weaker, smaller male cedes, and runs, fast,
away from the tree with the promising nesting hollow
and towards the pale blue house. He launches up the
wood siding, his claws digging into the flaking paint,
finding easy purchase in the soft old wood, winching
his way upwards: forelegs first together as a pair, then
hind, thighs powering upwards, all the way to the roof.
He's been here before, knows he cannot get in. This
house, unlike most, has been rigged to prevent entry
from outside. There is old wire, old but strong, still
blocking the likely entry ways along the gutters. At the
vent is a substantial metal grate. He knows he cannot

get in here either, but pauses on the shady side of the roof, scrabbles fast and optimistic at a roof shingle, is disappointed when he cannot lift it, but unsurprised. He scurries along the roof and leaps, a satisfying high leap with his legs spread wide, to the next tree, one webbed unpleasantly by spiders and caterpillars. He will have to keep looking for a nesting place.

He keeps moving.

Sweetness and time. Gentle now: boughs, squirrels, even the roofs themselves.

DANNY

After her fall, her plunge downwards to carpet, earth, floor, Linnie was not right. She couldn't cry. Sometimes she couldn't keep her tongue in her mouth properly and the saliva would drool out.

Ma took her to Saint Joseph's hospital the afternoon of the fall, and a doctor studied Linnie. Ma told him the baby had fallen off the change table. He said there was a concussion and nothing else. But in the weeks that followed it was clear there was more than concussion. There were "complications." Back at the hospital, after more tests, doctors said maybe there had been damage, a small stroke perhaps, or bruising in the brain itself, but that Linnie was young and the brain was an amazing thing: she would heal.

Months went by and she did not heal. She did not ever again roll over, nor did she learn to crawl. She did not cry out loud, though sometimes tears would stream down her cheeks. She did not learn to say "Mama." At Johns Hopkins Hospital, a supposedly better hospital, doctors advised Ma that Linneah presented with more symptoms than could possibly be the result of a single fall. They implied the child had been beaten, or dropped repeatedly, or shaken. Social workers came to our house and interviewed us, as well as our neighbors. The police came, and interviewed all of those people again. They told Ma they were keeping a record so that if there were other suspicious "events" they would investigate as though it were a criminal case.

Ma cried at night, holding Linnie, ashamed that so many people could believe she was capable of brutalizing her own baby. Finally, not quite satisfied that Ma wasn't beating Linnie, but unable to prove that she was, the doctors and social workers concluded that there must have been damage in utero, or congenital damage, for more was wrong with Linnie than they could explain.

In my heart, I knew it *was* all my fault. She had been fine before the fall.

Linnie got worse, but Ma wouldn't take her back to the hospitals because she was afraid they would take Linnie away, that social workers would take me away, and that perhaps the police would take her away too. She was scared. So Linnie's drooling got worse, and she had seizures, and we didn't do anything for her but hold her. Ma missed days of work at the Legion. She was going to get fired. Her boss would call and Ma would be afraid to say the baby was sick, because the social workers and police had talked to her boss as well, so she would say instead that *she* was feeling unwell. Her boss would yell down the phone that Ma must have a drinking problem or something and that she should get herself to an AA meeting. Or maybe she was pregnant again but how could that be because John was gone on duty, right? Ma would inhale deeply. She'd respond "No, Sir" and "Yes,

Sir" and "I'll be there tomorrow, don't you worry, Sir" while I held Linnie and stroked her.

At night, Ma stood in the front room, looking out the French doors to the porch, rocking Linnie and crying. She smoothed her hand over the baby's face, and Linnie watched her fingers, intent on them. Ma ran a finger down the baby's nose, over her wet lips, over and over again. She rubbed gently the space between Linnie's eyebrows, where there was a pair of moles that looked, I was to learn later when I learnt a bit of German, just like an umlaut, and then bent to kiss that place, tenderly.

Impact: a sudden blow.

An adult voice, a man, yelling.

A boy cries, and then, white-blond in the spring moonlight, he stumbles into the yard. He runs to its furthest corner and curls up in the hollow, weeping, his tears snot saliva running into my soil.

At the front of the house, a door slams, then a car chokes itself alive and leaves into the dark night.

Inside the fieldstone house, a woman sleeps too soundly through all this, falling down into her self-induced, pill-addled dreams.

A baby starts to cry inside, wailing like a lost cub, wailing on into the night for all the breezes long, for as long as a cloud to cross the night sky all the way from the moon to the horizon.

Finally, the white-blond boy stiffens under the moonlight, wipes his muddy tears on his pajama sleeve, gets up and goes inside. He returns with the small girl baby.

His white-blond hair, her grey eyes in the moonlight.

He curls in the hollow again, the baby nestled against his belly, cooing and happy as he dandles his fingers over her face for her to see.

Then both sleep, these pale cubs, curled in the palm of my hollow, under the clear spring moon, the scent of night lavender around them. When the fox trots along the alley she catches in the wind the scent of human close by and pauses, confused. She slinks closer, slides through the fence to see them. She stands on the lip of the hollow and sees the child and the baby, asleep as if two kits in a den, the baby girl sucking gently on the boychild's smallest finger.

The weather turned today. You can feel it, the bit of dry and cool that means finally the most uncomfortable summer heat is done with. It's a nice afternoon to be on the porch. Sun's still warm (but not too warm), it's still hot enough for iced tea and short sleeves, but I am not sweating. Nice. Tyrell is off with my mower. I let him borrow it. I know he is out mowing other people's yards for cash. It's what he does when he runs short. It's my mower, and he earns the money. I don't mind. If fall is coming as I feel it is, he needs to mow now. People's grass is going to stop growing.

I was up late last night, doing numbers for the car export place. The proprietors, two broad-shouldered black men with broad faces and strong accents, were suspicious about having me offer to be their accountant under the table when I showed up, laptop under my arm, but I let them give me some examples of foreign currency transactions they *might* do and ran it through my quick working up of Form 926, the stuff on foreign intermediaries and flow-throughs, and they were interested. They clearly had thought, from the look of me, that I was another black B'more addict. Really the slogan on the bus benches in Govans could be "B'more addicted" rather than "Baltimore: The Greatest City in America" or maybe, given the water mains and sewage lines that keep leaking and opening up messy sink holes into which whole streets, sidewalks and houses fall, "Baltimore: It's Going Down."

The Auto Export guys thought I wouldn't know a cedi from a beedi, a baht from a bong. That I knew the tax forms as well as the currencies stumped them. I showed them my 1992 accounting certificate from Baltimore City Community College. It was somewhat out of date, admittedly. Then I asked if they wanted to come outside and smoke a cigarette with me. When we were outside in the parking lot smoking Benson and Hedges I asked all about where they were from. Turns out are they are Côte d'Ivoirians fed up of being used car salesmen in West Baltimore and branching out into an independent tag/title and export business. I told them about my upbringing, living on Air Force bases with my step-father John. Philippines, Japan and Germany: I had gotten around a bit. I had never made it to Africa though. I wish I'd made it to Africa. John sent me back to the US when I was seventeen, and then it was either commit to my repatriation or enlist once I turned eighteen, and I didn't want to enlist.

Anyway, a little bit of explaining, a little bit of sharing while smoking the cigarettes I'd carefully bought even though I am not a regular smoker myself because I had a hunch these guys might be Africans, and Africans tend to be smokers in my experience. Bingo: a good result. I've socialized my way into nice lucrative international work to keep me happy into the wee hours.

So, three on a lovely end of summer afternoon and I am outside on my porch still only on my second iced tea of the day. I'm slow and happy, watching the traffic go by when Em walks up without her dogs, a six pack of beer dangling from her fingers by its plastic yoke.

"Hey" she says, from the front sidewalk.

"Hi there, Em! Where's the dogs at?"

"Hopefully not at your Mom's house!" she jokes. I guess the look on my face shows I don't find that funny, even though I'm trying to smile.

She looks away.

"No, really. They're home, safe. I wanted to come by and properly thank you for helping with my little dog a few weeks ago. I should've done this sooner." She holds up the Coors, six silver bullets: "For you."

Well, the thing with the dog was over a month ago. Anyway, I say, "Oh. Thanks, Em. Come on up. You want to sit a bit, have a beer? I'm drinking iced tea myself. I make it fresh each day. Real English Breakfast tea, no sugar. I have some anise cookies inside too."

"Uh. OK, yeah. Great. Iced tea would be nice actually. No cookies, thanks."

Em comes up, looks uncomfortable for a moment, hands me the six-pack and then sits, legs wide apart like a man, on the overturned Home Depot bucket which is typically Tyrell's perch out here, so I go in to get her tea and to fill up my own. I put the beer in the fridge, wondering if maybe Tyrell will like it or if I should pass it along to the guys at the corner store. Then I get a tall glass for Em and ladle us some tea out of my red and white enamel pot. It *is* good tea. Looseleaf. I walk all the way down to that new organic grocery store in Hampden to stock up once a month or so. Every day when I wake up I boil a big saucepan of water and add two tea-eggs full of leaves to it. Then I shut the heat off, leave a ladle in it and dish out tea all day. A handful of ice makes it extra nice! It smells like tea, not like dust. Some teabags just smell like dust. I put some *springerle* on a plate as well, just in case. Not everyone likes anise, but they go well with tea. I make a huge batch at Christmas to give away as the Germans do, fiddling with the little molds that made a wheat sheaf pattern on each one, but not many of my friends like them in spite of how delicate and pretty they look. Too German, too weird, not sweet enough, they say. Anyway, more for me, I guess. I still have a couple dozen in the freezer. Every week I defrost a few to go with my iced teas. I balance the plate of cookies on top of my glass, hold Em's glass in my other hand, and push the front door open with my ass, emerging backwards into the sunlight.

"Tea, and cookies, but Em don't say no to my cookies, alright? They aren't very sweet, they taste a bit like licorice, and I made them myself."

"You're a baker?"

"Only once a year. Then I do a big German cookie blow-out. Different kind of cookie every year. This year it was anise cookies. I froze a bunch, don't worry. These ones are nice and fresh still."

Em looks at me intently. Too hard. She takes her tea, sits down, stands up, takes a cookie, and then sits down again, heavily, all the while trying to read my face with those sharp grey eyes of hers. Holding the cookie and tea like she's already forgotten them, she blurts,

"Did you move to Germany then, when you were ten?"

Boy, she remembers the details. I guess I gave her ten when we were outside Ma's.

"Ha. Em. My goodness girl, you don't forget a thing, do you? No, not Germany right away. Philippines and Japan first. My step-father was in the Air Force."

"But, wait. Did your mother go overseas too?"

"No. They'd already split up by then."

Em looks confounded. She's too intent, still watching me too hard with her tea listing in her hand so much that it's going to spill. And then she backs right off, leans back, looks at the street. Pulls herself together, takes a visible deep breath.

"Sorry. I shouldn't be so nosy."

"It's OK. Tell me some about you."

"Well," as she sits up straighter, "I did go to Ghana with the Peace Corps."

Em left a little while after Tyrell showed up with the mower, heaving it up my front steps like it was a big dead pig. Our talk had gotten smoother after she tried the *springerle* and tea. Nothing like good food and drink to smooth a conversation, but it was still awkward. I started asking questions to try and figure out why she wants to know all about Ma's house so bad, but I can't say I've figured it out. She's got her own house, which has a big yard for those dogs, and is apparently mortgage free. However, she's a yoga teacher and she told me she can't afford to replace her grill that was stolen last month, so she can't have a ton of money. She's probably not looking to buy Ma's place. Probably. Maybe she's got a girlfriend somewhere who wants to buy it?

Anyway, Tyrell showed up and the three of us talked a bit, mostly about how Tyrell's mowing had gone (good, he did five properties this afternoon), and then they left.

So, I'm sitting here in the kitchen, alone in the last light of the day.

Hahn. I haven't thought about Hahn in a long time, and there it was on the tip of my tongue, German like the cookies. Hahn and before that Kadena and before *that* Luzon. *AFB, Baby.* The Air Force base years. Dug up out of my memory twice today, by talking to the Auto Export guys *and* again by that Em.

Me, Tom Bowman and Jimmy Carney laughing like wolves in the woods at night out on the far side of the airstrip, away from the school and the commissary and the overfull parking lot by the bank and fitness center. Away from the thousands of people at Hahn. Away from the base housing: squat apartment blocks that looked more communist than anything, each one just the same down to the indent in the concrete outside everyone's front door in which you were to supposed to place your doormat. Even the doormats, all purchased in the same stores, seemed to be all the same: *wilkommen* all the way down, door after door.

When the jets landed it sounded like the air ripping. You'd have to put your hands to your ears, even in the woods. Even in the woods the jet fuel smell would oil its way onto the back of your tongue, overpowering the earth smell of the cold night and mucky leaves. Funny how the birds got used to the planes. The air would vibrate, shaken so much it looked like you were seeing the world through wavy glass, and the birds would just keep on chirping: cuckoos in the trees, and sometimes a grouse smashing through the undergrowth.

Tom, Jimmy and Me. I was the best at math. I was friendly. I could get anyone to talk to me. At school, everyone would talk to me, teachers, students, even girls, because I liked asking questions, and most of all, I liked listening. People like to talk, if you'll listen. I didn't like to talk. My own voice always sounded weird to me. There wasn't an accent that fit me anymore: urban Baltimorean seemed like a far reach back to someone I didn't even want to be, and I wasn't Filipino or Japanese or German, *and* I wasn't the kind of white guy whose mouth was home to the Standard American English we were taught in the DOD schools. Worst of all, over the years I noticed that my accent would slide when I spoke to someone. I would start to adopt whatever their accent was, and if I didn't catch myself, I'd even start mimicking their hand gestures. It embarrassed me. What if someone noticed? What if they thought I was making fun of them? It was better to ask a couple of good questions and then shut up.

It was senior year and Tom was set to go to the University of Illinois for college the next fall, while Jimmy was planning to enlist and be a pilot like his dad. I had no plans. Mr. Sherrer, our math teacher, wanted me to apply to some of the big names: *Harvard* he said, *Columbia.* He said I should do math or computing. It was like he didn't even notice my skin, like my blackness was no impediment, nor was my being from a poor-ass family from Baltimore. He just thought I was smart and I should go.

Jimmy, Tom and Me, laughing in the woods at night, like wolves. We had scored some weed in Lautzenhausen from a guy outside the Dolly Bar. *Ya, bitte!* Our first purchase, an exorbitantly overpriced, tightly rolled little joint. What fun. We coughed our inexperience into the dark trees and cold air, coughed trying to get smoke into our lungs, coughed inhaling the jet fumes, and burnt our lips when they clutched the skinny, soggy spliff as we held our hands over our ears to block out the cleaving air cacophony of take off or landing. *Night maneuvers*, suddenly hilarious.

It was all hilarious until Tom's sister, Helen, curly-haired, broad-hipped, younger than her brother by a year and angry about life, found us in the woods:

"*Dad's* home." She snarled at her brother. Tom started to laugh, but it sounded like the hilarity that comes with unexpected fear.

"Dad is home, and he has been waiting since 17:40. He wants us all to report for chores. He's got the duty roster out."

"Oh Shiiiiiit!" laughed Tom. "Shit!" gulping in air that made the laugh sound a bit like a sob. "Shit! I forgot."

It was 18:30, six thirty: for a man with a short temper fifty minutes was a very long time to wait.

Tom and Helen scarpered off through the woods and Jimmy and I stayed. The joy was gone out of our escapade but we loitered in the woods anyway, kicking at the fall leaves, kind of cold, unsure what to do next. I wasn't all that worried for myself, but clearly Tom was about to have something terrible happen to him. First, he was late and, though hopefully his Dad wouldn't notice, second he was a little stoned, just the little you could get from one ineptly smoked, shared spliff.

In our apartment over in housing (the "slum" as some called it), John never noticed much if I was there or not, even if I missed meals. Mary would leave me something to eat; she'd have it waiting for me on the table under an overturned mixing bowl. Sometimes she'd balance a chocolate bar, something American from the commissary, a Mars or Kit Kat bar, or a stack of three Oreos, on top of the bowl. She was thoughtful with these little treats. She liked to leave me something I liked. It made me feel young and foolish, but I did like it. She didn't mind what time I came back. She'd probably be drinking iced tea and reading one of the Filipino magazines from the big box her family sent her every quarter, to keep her in touch with her home country and with Luzon while she was on yet another far away posting with John. Sometimes I would look them over too.

Luzon was where I had moved in with John. It felt like a dream, having ever been there. Sometimes Mary would open one of those boxes of magazines from her Philipines home and a smell would come off them that I recognized: ink and cheap paper when they have caught some damp heat. It would feel like a horse had kicked me in the chest, that smell. Overwhelming, familiar and so utterly from another place, another time, that it made me feel like there must have been *another me*, someone else altogether who had lived in Luzon and seen the palm fronds, the glossy banana leaves.

Ma had begged him to take me. Ma never even met Mary, but knew that if John was remarrying he would get family housing on base, and that I could be with him. She wanted me out of Baltimore. After Linnie, I just couldn't get myself right.

Back in Baltimore, Linnie fell, then Linnie was dead, and I was a criminal hiding in my own life. I wouldn't go to school, and Ma couldn't face me, never mind force me to do anything. Sometimes she would walk to school with me, the two of us silent and side by side. She'd give me a perfunctory peck on the crown of my head, and watch me go in the front door. I'd slip out the side, or out the bathroom window. She could go to work after Linnie died, in fact she was an exemplary worker: never missed another day. She even picked up extra every time her boss called. He would congratulate her on "kicking the juice or whatever, honey" and she, invisible to him on her end of the line, would cringe.

I never went up to the Legion anymore, not like I'd used to with Linnie. I'd just sit at the back of our house whittling sticks into sharp spears, or run away, up to hide on the grounds of Tivoli, Pratt's old mansion, if anyone came looking. I'd try to work for my lunch at the commune on Woodbourne. They called themselves "The Institute for Social Research" and wouldn't let me hang out in their yard. I was surprised by how strict they were: you didn't chip in, you didn't hang out, and they didn't want or need a little truant. They didn't rat me out though, and if I did some of the more unpleasant jobs for them (like climbing into their attic to chase away the squirrels nesting in it, which was a job I already knew pretty well from doing it at home), they'd let me share lunch with them: big vegetable soups and salads with greens from their own garden, and thickly buttered store-bought brown bread from Pantry Pride.

Back in those Baltimore days when John was still Ma's husband, he'd come home on leave from the war, brusque and simmering with rage. He laid into Ma for letting me run wild. "Jojo! He's your son. Look after him!" he'd yell. And Ma would yell back "You adopted him when we got married. He's your boy too. You help him!" Linnie's death was something Ma never elaborated on with John. I don't think she ever fully explained. Maybe he never asked. His head was full of 'Nam and its terrors and tragedies, so the tragedy of his own baby's death didn't touch him so much. He never knew her. He'd been away at war for the whole life of his daughter. Thankfully, he never asked to go the grave, because there wasn't one.

"Jesus, Joanne! Do something about that boy. I can't stand him being here all the time, doing shit-all all day long, looking stupid!" But Ma couldn't do anything about me. Or rather, she was doing all she could. I saw that she was trying to keep me safe in spite of what I'd done. She was trying to be my mother in spite of being unable to look me in the eye.

There were actually lots of things John couldn't stand when he came home: the house with its untidy piles of pamphlets and church newsletters on the coffee table, unmowed lawn and dirty plates in the sink; Ma's dresses ("Do you have to wear an apron? A scarf on your hair? You look like a slave from a hundred years ago"); and most of all Ma's religion. Over the course of the war, she had become more devout, and he had lost his faith entirely.

There was lots she didn't like either: his blaspheming, his anger, his violent attempts to make the house run like it was a branch of the military. He left for his next deployment and didn't come back.

By 1973 I was ten, and still trouble. I got caught stealing from the grocery store. I got Ma in trouble because I wouldn't go to school regularly. I even made the folks at the commune mad when I broke a bunch of plates, on purpose but without explanation, one afternoon. That year John called my mother from the Philipines to ask for a divorce so he could marry Mary, a Filipino woman. I heard the call, Ma's side of it anyway, and the jump of hope in her voice as she must have realized that married, with a new wife, and base housing for a family rather than a single man, he could change our lives:

"Sure thing. You send me the papers; I'll sign. I only want one thing from you. Just one thing. Take Danny. I know. It's far, and not so easy over there. I know. But folks at the Legion tell me the schools on bases are good. The boy needs a change. He needs help. He needs to go to school. He needs not to be here, John. Please John. Please. You adopted him, so he's legally a dependent. He can go. He can live on base with you . . . and what's her name? Oh. Mary? Is she Catholic? He can live with you and Mary. It'd do him good not to be here. He'll be better there, I'm sure of it. Please John. I won't ask for anything else, no money, none of your pension. Please help Danny."

So, I was packed off to Clark Air Base on Luzon Island in the Philipines to live with Catholic Mary and non-believer John: *Mabuhay Clark Air Base*. To my surprise, he let his new wife hang a lurid wooden crucifix over their bed: the blood dripping from Jesus's feet and wrists suspended right over their stark white polyester pillowcases. I still hated John, and he was still strict, martial at home like it was an extension of work. But even in those early years when she hardly knew me, Mary was a good thing. She was a sweet, tiny woman, with cheeks that dimpled when she giggled, which she did a lot. She was young too, maybe twenty; she liked sweets as much as I did. She had lots of younger siblings, plus nieces and nephews. She talked about them all the time. She was easy with me. She knew how to be with a ten year-old, and she didn't know about what I'd done.

The other Air Force wives weren't kind to her though. They themselves were a mix of women, white and black, who would have been poorer and more powerless stateside than they were on base overseas. Buoyed by their husbands' ranks, the wives of Majors, Captains and Chief Master Sergeants, they could be aloof about Mary (wife of a lowly Senior Master Sergeant) and not invite her to their potluck dinners. They liked gossiping about how John might have met her too: she was so young and so local. Had she been his whore one night on the town? Had she trapped him somehow, maybe by feigning a pregnancy? Poor fool him, they laughed, sometimes intentionally just within Mary's earshot at the base club. Consequently, Mary matured over the years, giggled less. The casual xenophobia of the Air Force wives made her bitter. She stayed sweet to me though, always kind. She never really loved me, but she was never mean either. I was fed pretty good meals, and I went to the school on base where I was treated just like everyone else. It took me a while to catch up, but I did.

From Luzon to Kadena, Japan and from Kadena to Hahn, Germany. Different countries that I got to know a little bit, even though the bases themselves were all remarkably alike, miniature Americas with commissaries stocking fruit loops, and movie theaters showing American films for a buck fifty a show: *Jaws, One Flew Over the Cuckoo's Nest, Star Wars.*

Generally, the rigidity of base life was good for me. It was highly structured. At the end of the duty day, the loudspeakers would play the national anthem and every kid obediently stopped playing or running or yelling to reverently hold their hand on their heart and stand still until it was over. I had no freedoms, but neither did anyone else. I was far from Baltimore. I could start over. I became the friendly kid. I got great at math. At each of John's new postings, I hit those parts of my identity harder. By Hahn, I was The Friendliest Kid, and The Best at Math. Those good things hid my past from others. My life philosophy comes from that time, from those transitions and chances to remake myself: be so upbeat, cheerful and friendly that you make people's days better. Maybe if you make enough days better for the people around you, you can forgive yourself.

Will called my father Brian, and so I always did too. Brian ran his own dental practice, and could set his own hours. He always took Fridays off so that he could go out on his boat, a ten foot aluminum power boat he kept in Essex. He'd take it up Middle River and meander along the shallow, weed-thick creeks that fed into it. He fished to get away from us; Will and I certainly were never invited along and Birdie was too fastidious to want to "sit in mucky water all day" so she never went either. Sometimes Brian would come home with a bucket of bony sunfish or a big bass. Usually though, he'd just come home with a sunburn and a tolerant mood that might last him through the weekend if we were lucky. In order to get those Fridays off, he and Birdie worked seven am to six pm Monday through Thursday.

Their work hours meant us kids needed to get to school and back by ourselves. When I was seven and eight, and he was fourteen and fifteen, it was Will's job to walk me to and from school. I was enrolled in Roland Park Country School, which was all girls; he was enrolled at Gilman, the private boys' school across the street. Separated by the generous leafy boulevard on Roland Avenue, the schools faced each other as if in an irresolvable debate profoundly underscored by gender bias. Uniforms? RPCS says yes (blue tunics or skirts, white blouses: we looked like airline hostesses), Gilman says no (a dress code requiring khakis, shirt and tie: they looked like young executives). Sports? RPCS says ok (but also arts and music and free play and gardening: build your womanly skills, girls), Gilman says at least one hour of vigorous team sport every day (gentlemen, build your connections: it's not what you know, it's who you know). My school liked to brag of its distant and romantic affiliation with the Bonapartes, built as it was on land once owned by Charles, the great grandson of Jerome, who was Napoleon's brother. Will's school liked to brag of its affiliation with the eminent Johns Hopkins University, as it once occupied Homewood House on what became the Hopkins Homewood campus.

Both schools began admitting African-American students in the late sixties, but when I went, RPCS was still a pretty *white* place. Ostensibly, it was very open-minded. Financially it was pretty elitist. I concealed my Dad's occupation from my friends Lynn and Sabina. Lynn vaguely knew her father did something "in finance" and Sabina's father travelled all the time doing some kind of medical research. I said my Dad was a surgeon, but was unspecific about what kind. *He does surgery sometimes*, I thought to myself, justifying the lie. Oral surgery is still surgery, right?

It took Will and me about an hour each way to walk to and from school, because we dilly-dallied. Will let me pick flowers out of people's fancy yards, we threw helicopter seeds at each other, and when we crossed Stony Run, we'd take our shoes and socks off and play in the creek, no matter what season it was. After school we'd stop at Eddie's and buy enormous pastries. I favored the cinnamon buns, dripping with white icing. Will liked the cherry Danish with its lurid red filling.

I tried doing the walk on my own when Will didn't want to walk with me anymore, when he had his new friends. It was easy. I had walked the route so many times before. It was boring on my own though, so I started experimenting with different ways to get home. I tried cutting through Notre Dame's campus, which had a big steep hill down from its stately red brick buildings to the creek, and I tried heading all the way down to Coldspring, which was too loud with traffic; I didn't like that route so much. One day I thought to cut straight across Charles Street, through Homeland with its pretty ornamental duck ponds, clear through to York Road.

York Road was roaring with traffic, the air thick with dust. When I arrived at York and Woodbourne and looked up from the pavement, my nine year old self in her blue and white school uniform was the only white person in sight. York road was teeming with people; it was like arriving unexpectedly in a foreign country. *I have come to a city in Africa!* I thought. I was scared, and excited. I loved it. A man was yelling loudly to another man across the street and I couldn't understand either of them. It didn't even sound like English to me. A rotund older woman with dark circles under her dark eyes and heavy plastic shopping bags in each hand stepped off the sidewalk into the traffic to move around me, where I had stopped still on the pavement. She said "excuse me, Miss," so deferentially that I was embarrassed. I got confused about directions. I crossed York and kept going on Woodbourne. I walked a ways and got more scared because although there were fewer people there were also no landmarks I recognized. It baffled me: how could a place so utterly unfamiliar and wonderful be walking distance from the school? From my house? Where the hazelnuts *was* I?

A car pulled up next to me, orange with a big bulbous back window. A young white man with long sandy hair flopped over his shoulders and his bangs in his eyes rolled his window down, his cranking arm moving fast:

"Kid. You lost?" I knew I looked as out of place as I felt.

He drove me home. I sat in the deep bucket of his car's front seat, wishing I could see over the dashboard more easily. I tried not to stare at his tie-died shirt. Birdie wouldn't let Will or me wear tie die.

Birdie and Brian were both home by the time I got there.

"No good fucking hippie commune pot-heads," Brian cursed after the floppy haired tie-die man had left.

After that I had to take the school bus.

Rain last night. When I let the dogs out in the yard early this morning, getting ready for our walk, the grass is heavy with water droplets, round and shining in the very first greyness of morning light. It smells of moist soil. There's a mourning dove pacing on the flagstone patio, nervous as it walks its circles. Its grey plumage shivers with auburn and rose up to the bird's delicate face, dark eyes and beak. Grandpa used to say these doves were mourning for Betsy, poor Betsy.

Once upon a time, somewhere around forty-third street, there had been a racetrack where the horse hooves would cut the soil and their hoofbeats would drum hearts to passion. Young Betsy met handsome Jerome, Napoleon Bonaparte's brother, as hooves of passion were drumming past them. They loved, they married, they sailed to Europe where Jerome bought silver and gold muslins for his beautiful young bride, imagining the dresses that would flatter her ample bosom and emphasize the high flush of her cheeks. She was a *sexy* young woman: her father didn't approve.

In fact her father, wealthy William Patterson, hated his daughter, ostensibly for causing him more trouble than all his other children, his sons, all combined. (Really though he hated her for the improper stirring her beauty caused below his own waist, and he hated her also for her sharp words, which even he could see marked her as by far the smartest of all his other children, his sons, all combined).

Jerome's declarations of love for this pretty young American were as ineffectual as they were effusive: on its own good blue soil, France would not admit Betsy to the Royal family. She, and her young son Bo (Jerome Bonaparte Jr.), were sent back to Baltimore, rejected. France declared the marriage *nul.* Betsy had to move back into her father's house: the shame and frustration of it burned her very soul.

Grandpa said on the day Betsy received the letters about Jerome's remarriage, she was wearing a dress with European silver muslin at the bodice, grey with a luminescent sheen of pink and red. She wore a comb in her hair with tear drop shaped amethysts rounded by tiny seed pearls. As she subsided to the earth, weeping, fabric billowing around her, the doves sat with her, taking on her plumage and her sadness, mourning. On their wings, the tear-drop shapes of the amethysts. *Oh! Coo coo coo.* Poor Betsy, they said. Poor Betsy.

But Betsy, she was feisty. She stood up abruptly, brushed the dust off her gown, and went inside to request that her handmaid (a surprisingly artistic and talented young woman) paint a scene on her chamber pot:

"I want it to show me, as beautifully as you can render me, and Jerome. He should be trying to kiss me, and I should be shoving him away. Paint him in that stupid wig of his with the tight little white curls that make him look like a poodle. Idiot man. Make him look as short as that domineering brother of his. Oh, Jerome! What a *bigamist*. If he is on my chamber pot, I will remember, every time I lift my skirts, that they shall never again admit such a vile and selfish dimwit, royalty or no.

Also, fetch someone to teach me about investing. I must have my own means. I will."

The dove on my patio sees its mate high above in the branch of the tulip poplar and, relieved, takes flight to meet it.

DANNY

Jimmy and I were throwing rocks at the trees in the dark when Tom's Dad found us. He had a massive cube of a flashlight, like a car battery with a headlamp on the front of it, and he swung its beam through the dark trees until he saw us. There was no point in running: he knew who we were, where we lived, and who our fathers were.

"You little *fucks*," he yelled, leaning into the motes caught in the white light, and for a moment his gaping yell was shot through with flashlight and you could see the inside of his cheek lit blood red like a living Halloween lantern.

At home, John was waiting for me, the veins in his neck already standing out: Tom's Dad had told him about the weed. Mary, who was herself scared of John's temper, was not home when I got there. Her spot on the couch was empty. The floral coaster on the coffee table was there, but no iced tea glass: there'd be no help from her.

John was icy and vicious, leaning across the dining table, his hands just inches from a metal mixing bowl under which my dinner presumably sat and on top of which was perched a fun-size snickers bar: "No way, Danny. There is *no way* I will tolerate this kind of behavior."

"No, sir." I kept my head down.

"You look at me, boy!"

"Yes, sir."

"Don't give me no attitude, you hear?"

"Yes, sir."

"No drug fiends in my house, you hear?"

"Yes, sir."

"None of this bullshit that'll get me in trouble. Reflect bad on me, on the mission. You hear?"

"Yes, sir."

"This is no Okinawa and you aren't with the red-neck Marines!"

In comparing me to the Marines, he had reached the pinnacle of his outrage. In Kadena two years ago there had been the incident on the beach over at Torii. Two US Marines, yelling and brawling drunk, decided to sleep on the beach, thinking to use dried ribbons of seaweed to make themselves a fire down by the water. They brought some local women over with them, to keep them company as they drank more and the fire smoked damply, as did their other kind of weed. The stories coming out of that night had been contradictory and depended a lot on whether you listened to the Okinawans or to US forces, but I guess the women were actually only fifteen year olds, and they claimed the men raped them. The upshot was that all American forces in Okinawa—Marines and Air Force—had a curfew imposed on them. That only made the Air Force more convinced than ever that the Marines were despicable lunk-heads.

"No reefer-smoking drug-dealing criminality in my house."

"It was just once—"

"Don't lip me, boy"

"But it was the only time! We'd never before. Some German guy by the Dolly Bar. He had just this one joint—"

John had swiftly rounded the table, his angry footfalls making the metal bowl on it rattle. With a flat open palm like a board of wood he smacked me, his arm swinging diagonally upwards so the impact started at my jawbone and sent the force through my molars, crushing them together.

"You're mighty lucky that wasn't my fist, boy."

I was holding my jaw.

"Shut up, now. And go to your room while I think what to do about you."

By the end of the weekend, I was on a flight out with a duffle bag of everything I could call my own. I was supposed to go to Ma. I was supposed to go back to that Alhambra house. I couldn't do it. John had given me twenty dollars: I blew it all on a cab from BWI to the Legion. I met Ma there, got money from her, and ignored her tears, ignored her grey hair, the new forward slope to her shoulders, like time was eroding her. I ignored my desire to hug her, to collapse into her and cry like a child.

I couldn't go back to living in that house.

I got money from Ma, and took a bus down York Road all the way to the Motel 6 on North Avenue, trying the whole way not to look foreign, trying to look as if the landscape, the place, wasn't some sort of familiar surprise, trying not to stare at the place as if it was the set of my own personal horror movie.

Em

By sixteen, Will had run away three times. I remember it as being all about the drugs and Will's menacing drug-friends. It seems now, looking back, there must have been more driving Will to the drugs than the drugs themselves. It's hard for me to remember the details. There was yelling, things never right between Will and Brian, Birdie intervening too much, or not enough. I am not sure how much of all that conflict I saw, misunderstood, and have somehow schooled myself to forget, or how much I just didn't see. Will told me that there were injuries, hospital visits. Birdie's hand did have a long scar across its back that Will claimed was a result of some drunken fight with Brian that he blundered into and tried to stop from happening. I don't remember. That fight might have happened when I was three or four; Will would have been ten or eleven. Will says he was the more frequent target when Brian was drunk, but I don't remember.

The fourth time Will ran away, he was seventeen and my parents didn't call the police. This meant that by my eleventh birthday I lived in the house as, essentially, an only child, and I was, guiltily, relieved. No more scary Will. No more horrible Will-friends. I had memories of my nice big-brother Will and I missed him, I missed that Will, profoundly. Yet I felt safer every day after school with Will gone. Sometimes I was scared he'd turn up unexpectedly, maybe with Mike or the guy with the gun tattoo. I'd get off the school bus and hold my breath, scaring myself, terrified, planning my steps to the phone to call Mom if he was there, or maybe to call the police. But he never was. He didn't come back to that house again until Dad, Brian, had died.

Mom and Dad lived in that Kerneway house their whole married lives. Then while out on his fishing boat my father died of an aneurism, a surge of blood like an unexpected deep swelling ocean wave that swept quick and obliterating through his skull. Mother went into assisted living for a brief spell until her kidneys truly gave out on her, and in the midst of organizing her cremation and funeral, I moved back home.

Em

I've woken out of a weird dream: shimmering blue and gold light on a tiled floor. In the dream I can hear water dripping in the background and my arms swing loosely as I pivot in circles, spinning and spinning. As I go round and round, I can see flashes of a window with a tree outside, a tub with shadowy water in it, a sink and a mirror. In that mirror over the sink I see glimpses of a middle-aged black woman with her eyes shut.

I can't shake the feeling the dream left me with: a vertigo in my gut. It's Tuesday. Traffic will be horrendous on York, even at six a.m., and yet I want to walk the Alhambra route, so I get the harnesses on the dogs and off we go. When we've fought through the bad-smelling exhaust air and commuter traffic to finally get to Danny's Ma's house, I don't care who sees me, and I don't understand why I feel the way I do. I stand on the sidewalk outside and cry, dog leashes in my right hand, my left hand covering my face while I hunch my shoulders and lean into grief. Girlfriend stands to the side looking uncertain. Blue repeatedly nudges the back of my knee with his damp nose and huffs, asking what I am doing. After a few minutes I stand up straight, look at the house, lean a hand down to Blue's back to reassure him, and then start walking.

When we get home, there's a message on my cell

phone, which I left on the counter because I never want it to ring at me when I'm out walking: that's private time. The little red light blinks to alert me, and I am irritated, I try to ignore it. I don't need a call today; I don't need anything unexpected. I still feel off-kilter, unhinged. I feed the dogs, give them fresh water, put the kettle on to boil. Phones never bring good news; there's always something stressful I don't want to deal with. Certainly in the last years of Mother's life, any call was bad news: she was sicker, there was a problem, there was an urgent new health care bill that I needed to deal with. Phone calls came with the weight of unexpected, unwanted, unrewarding, and frequently time-consuming responsibilities. I wait till after I've made and consumed tea and toast before I touch the screen on my phone.

Will. Will called me at six fifty-seven a.m. What the hell? I haven't heard from him at all this year, and his lifestyle doesn't exactly lend itself to early rising. Unless he's still up from the night before. That seems more likely. He's called from a number that's blocked, "unknown number," so I can't just call him back. His voice on the message is loud, quick, clear and he sounds cheerful, if agitated, addressing me by my childhood nickname, Pup. He said I always acted like a puppy. As a grown woman I cringe a bit at the diminution it implies, even though I know it's not what Will intends:

"Oh, Hey Pup! Sorry to call so early early. But hey hey, it's a beautiful day and I'm over at the McDonald's drinking coffee! Want to come join me? I'm going to be here til, uh, til eight thirty or so. You could buy me an egg sandwich. It'd be great!"

At least he's honest: he wants me to meet him so I'll buy him the egg sandwich he can't afford. It's unlike him to venture north of downtown. I wonder if Glenwood or the Jai medical center open at eight thirty. Is he up here for methadone? Or for some new injury? It's already eight fifteen.

I take the car so I'll be there faster, even though the York Road McDonalds is easy walking distance from Kerneway Ave. By the time I arrive, there's no sign of Will. I buy a coffee and sit, looking out the window, scanning the sidewalks for him, but I don't see him. I take the coffee with me and cross the street to look in the lobby of the Jai medical center: no sign.

I walk up to the Glenwood center. They don't open until ten. I don't know where Will is. There are a couple of churches east of York that offer food and refuge for the homeless, but much as I want to see Will, I don't feel like searching them. I wonder what he wanted. I offer my coffee—I haven't drunk a sip—to a skinny older black woman at the bus stop and she says, politely, "no thank-you" so I throw it away, then walk back to my car in the McDonald's parking lot. Maybe I could have driven Will somewhere this morning, after I'd offered him an Egg McMuffin. It's been a while since he's been in my car.

When I get into my little Hyundai I notice it has a

doggy funk smell to it. I reach to put the keys in the ignition and start the engine, but change my mind, pull my hand back into my lap and just sit there, watching the traffic stream past on York Road. Last time Will was in my car was when I drove him to see Mom, about a year before she died. She was in an assisted living facility in Lutherville, with an MD Mobility bus taking her to dialysis appointments every other day. Her private room tried to look like an apartment but still felt more like a hospital room, with its easy to mop linoleum floors and the narrow bed which had rails on the sides, like any hospital bed. It could be raised or lowered and could fold in the middle, lifting the head more, or elevating the knees so the legs could bend. She had a big window that didn't open and a desk under the window, which she never used. Along the back edge of the desk was a row of withering plants: red cyclamen, tired Christmas cactus, African violets. While she was there I visited every week, usually on a Thursday or Friday depending on her dialysis.

One time, just one time, Will came with me. He had shown up on my porch to ask for money just as I was heading over for a mid-afternoon visit with Mom; he looked clean, and though a bit wired seemed mostly coherent. Plus, it was cold outside, too cold for hanging around outdoors. He wouldn't come in to the house when I asked, so I suggested he come visit Mom with me. He agreed but then got nervous and weird about the visit once in my car, wondering if Mom would want to see him, asking me more than once if he should just get out at the next red light and catch the bus back into town. I kept reassuring him: Mom would be glad, we wouldn't stay long, and I would drive him wherever he wanted to go afterwards.

The whole drive there he fiddled with the knobs on my car radio, trying to get something other than NPR or top forty music out of it, critiquing WTMD, the alternative station, for playing too much blues music and not enough alt rock.

At one point I heard a sharp pop from his lap, followed by Will inhaling quick and hard.

"What was that?"

Will, cringing, holding his hand in his lap "My *nail.*"

"What?"

"My fingernail! It just snapped off." He held it up for me to see and I looked over quickly to catch a fleeting glimpse of the nail of his middle finger broken off way down low and blood pooling in the bed where the rest of the nail should have been.

The car swerved and I righted it, keeping my eyes on the road now,

"Shit! Jesus, Will. How'd you even *do* that? There're some napkins in the glove compartment."

"I was just. I. You know" as he fumbled in the glove box, letting the Hyundai owner's manual and service records that were tidily stored in there fall in a messy pile in his foot well.

"No, I don't know. What?"

"Just, you know. When you press the nails to see them go white? Checking to see if I am dehydrated."

"That's not how you check if you're dehydrated." I was annoyed about the paperwork that was now all over the floor, and spat the words. Plus, as a yoga teacher I felt I knew a lot about self-diagnosing ailments. As an addict, Will felt he knew a lot about how drugs affected humans. He too was annoyed and shot back:

"Yeah, Pups. You can. Too white means not enough circulation, and not enough circulation means not enough hydration." Then, trying to make light of it he added, "But pressing hard enough to break the nail? That means frustration, not hydration."

"Mm." I was unconvinced by his analysis, unamused by his rhyme, and annoyed. It made me think Will must be more high than I had realized if he could press his own finger hard enough to snap the nail. I was wishing more and more that I hadn't brought him.

When we got to Mom's residence, I saw the receptionist in the lobby take in the bloody beige Starbucks napkin wrapped around Will's middle finger. I saw her warily register *who* and *what* Will must be (a relative, sure, but also clearly an addict, and given all the vulnerable old folks up there with various kinds of meds, a huge *risk*). She gave me a significant look as she buzzed us through the glass doors to the elevator, a look that seemed to say "he's your responsibility. Keep him in check up there."

It was a change from what I typically thought I saw behind the standard greeting and smile; I always thought the nurses really wanted to ask "why haven't you visited yet this week?" I always felt embarrassed and ashamed when I came here. A once a week visit seemed like a lot to me when I tried to fit it into my schedule, but it never seemed to be enough, or even close to enough, when I was actually at the nursing home, confronted by the reality of this place and the dozens of hours my mother and other residents like her spent on their own. Will's oblivious jittery bouncing on the balls of his feet just added a new layer. I wished my family and I weren't such fuck-ups.

Fifth floor. Mom's room, her "apartment," is past the nursing station on this floor. There's no one at the nursing station and I am glad. Will, nervous and probably also far too high to be here, is talking way too loud. I am trying to block him out, ignore him. So many of the residents here are lonely women. The private apartments mostly have their doors open to the hall, and as we walk past you can see the small lives that cling in these small spaces: scrawled pictures drawn by grandchildren, framed photographs, an afghan carefully folded across the one easy chair in the room, a dusty vase with a fake flower in it, a metal cane with a tripod at its base for extra stability, a walker, a wheelchair.

We get to Mom's room. She's up, not in bed, which

is always a good sign. Someone has braided her hair in a long pigtail down her back, a style she never wore before living here. She's seated in the one easy chair, watching TV, CNN, the news announcing itself loudly in the cramped space. I stand where she can easily see me. Will sprawls on her bed, rumpling the blankets. He looks too big there, too much like the outside world is alive on him, grimy, bloody napkin still on his finger. He's still talking way too loud. He lounges, propped up on his elbow, for a moment and then bounces up again to give Mom a kiss on the cheek. Mom is delighted to see him. She is so happy the tears stream down her face. She stands, not quite up straight: it's like her hips are locked into seated position, perpetually ready to sit, never to walk. I just want to be out of there. The TV keeps talking. It's always awkward to see Mom, and having Will here, being weird, is excruciating. I am settling myself, leaning against the wall, trying to just be still, but it turns out it is Will who can't deal.

"OK, Pups" he announces after only being there for ten minutes, "I am going to find a bathroom and then shall we go?"

"You can use my bathroom," Mom chimes. Will looks and sees her bathroom is a toilet and shower in a tastefully wall-papered enclosure that doesn't have a door.

"Nah. I saw one in the hall. I'll be right back."

While he's gone, I ask Mom what breakfast had been,

what was for lunch, when her next dialysis is (tomorrow, obviously, if it wasn't today, but I ask anyway), and if she needs anything. "New socks" she says, even though I had just brought her new socks last week. I go to the drawer and show her the Fruit of the Loom tube socks, unopened. "No" she says, shaking her head, annoyed, full of effort, "not *white*. Those are awful. Get me black socks. Easy to put on socks. I have trouble bending you know."

I am exasperated, but nod. Easy to put on? *No* socks are easy to put on if you can't bend. I will bring black socks next time I come.

Will comes back and we leave, precipitously, Mom looking stricken at our quick departure. Will walks so fast down the hall to the elevator that I have to jog to keep up. He goes quickly all the way to my car. It is only once we are inside that Will starts to laugh: high coughing giggles, somewhere between a feral dog and a cartoon one. It's a naughty teenage boy laugh and it is out of place on a lumpy man in his forties. He pulls a box of Russell Stover chocolates out from under the flap of his coat.

"What the fuck, Will! Where'd you get those?"

He's still laughing as he takes the lid off.

"She was sleeping! Old biddy a couple over from Mom. Mouth wide open and false teeth hanging half out! I swiped them from her table. Here."

I push the box away, disgusted, and start to drive.

I head onto the beltway. I am planning a quick trip into the city: 695 to 83-south, to wherever Will wants to go. He's talking, non-stop, eating chocolates as he talks, pushing two or three at a time into his mouth and talking through the slurry made by their cream fillings mixed with his saliva. On and on he talks about how last time he was in rehab he'd had to do therapy. He monologues about how his childhood was the root of all his problems, how Mom wouldn't let Dad (my dad, not his) parent him, about the detrimental effects of having Mom cut off his contact with his own real father. On and on Will goes. He tells me that when he was fourteen one of Mom's dental hygienist friends hit on him. "She was, like, thirty. And she tried to kiss me!" He is appalled at his own suffering. I am appalled too. I love my brother. I want to love my brother. But here, in the car, eating stolen chocolates, lips messy with it, I can't stand him. I want more reconciliation, less awkwardness. I want to be in his life more, but right then I just want to stop the car on the side of the highway and run screaming off into the traffic.

"Mike Talermo touched me between the legs in the bathroom," I interrupt.

Will pauses for a moment, looks hard at me, and then continues his rant about things he has said to therapists, like I never said anything.

I tune out. I think Mom *did* try to sustain Will's relationship with his father. I remember Tim coming to take Will on vacation, at least once. Somewhere there are photos: a beach, Tim and Will and a sandcastle. When did that happen? How old was Will in those photos? Nine maybe? I don't know. I also remember, oddly, or it seems odd because as an adult I'd never really given it much consideration before, trips Will took to stay with his Dad in the countryside, and with his Dad's new wife Kathy. These were trips that *I also went on.* As Will rants, and I drive, I marvel at those foggy memories: what was that all about? Tim and Kathy take Will *and me*, the child of Birdie's new relationship? What was that like for Tim? What was that like for Kathy? Whose idea was it that I go along?

I remember that Tim was a Computer Scientist for Hopkins, back when all that technology was newfangled and impressive. I remember Tim's preference for being barefoot outside (fastidious Birdie must have hated that). I remember that Kathy's Mom joined us on vacation and that I loved her. I called her Omi Bye (I don't remember if that reflected her real name). She was being treated for cancer and wore a wig to cover her bald head; she showed it to me so I wouldn't be scared of it. Once when I had a sore throat she made me slice after slice of white bread and margarine, the kind of sweet fluffy melt in your mouth bread Germanic Birdie couldn't tolerate, but I loved. I must have only been four or five. I loved Omi Bye.

That trip to Ma's nursing home was the last time Will was in my car: a winter years ago.

Finally I leave the McDonalds parking lot and drive home. I sit in the Hyundai, parked outside my house, in the shade, and for the second time this morning I cry into my hands.

Teaching at Mid-Town later is a relief. As I walk up the stairs from the street to the studios and unlock the front door I can take on my yoga-teacher self, and block out how unhinged I feel, how grief-stricken about not seeing Will. I can block out how desperate I feel about not being able to contact him and not knowing if or when he will contact me again. I sign in Jen and Alan, regulars at the eleven a.m. vinyasa class I teach.

I set out a single stick of incense to perfume the air, but not cloy it. I put on the Jai Uttal/Madonna playlist and I lay out four mats: one for myself at the front of the room, and three others for the inevitable late students so that they can come in and get started without being too disruptive. I like walking barefoot on the polished wood. I feel like I can inhale both the music and the incense and by doing so arrive at a bit of calm. These details are always the same when I set up here for class. Whatever other tumult is going on, this room is a stable place, its purpose constant and reliable. It's already pretty warm in studio A, and the class is vinyasa, not hot yoga, so I don't turn on the heater.

Jen probably shouldn't be doing the class as it looks from her rubbing of it and grimaces like she has a sore shoulder; Alan spends the pre-class time cheerfully showing off his ease with arm balances, doing handstands and crow-pose as the room fills. There are also two college girls who usually go to the ashtanga class in the evening –they are stong, fit, and like Jen and Alan a bit too competitive about their yoga prowess; Henry the determined and muscle-bound accountant; quiet Janine; two other young women, friends and new to the studio "but not new to yoga" they assure me; and today's delight: Heather.

I idolize Heather, one of the other midtown instructors. She studied with Richard Freeman in Boulder, and with Pattabhi Jois in Mysore. She knows so much, can do so much. She's strong and calm. She also has two young children and is not fashionably skinny: she's beautiful. She's got a long blond braid, an easy laugh, and no superior attitude even though of all of us, she deserves to feel superior.

We start class seated, breathing. Another regular, Melanie, always frazzled from her rushing around, and always rushing because she's frazzled, arrives a few minutes late and takes one of my late mat spots with a shrug and smile of apology. Inhale, exhale. Inhale, exhale. As class progresses, we link the breaths with movement, the phrasing and breathing rote to me: inhale reach up, exhale fold forward, inhale flat back, exhale chaturanga. Inhale, exhale. What a relief to be reminded of the animal human, that which can be reduced to breathing in and out, that which just carries on and doesn't strain towards ineffable things. Melanie is jittery and takes a while to settle in. Fortunately, she has taken the late mat near Heather, who is a steadying and yet inspiring model for those around her: her postures represent some of the miracles the human body can perform.

From downward dog (in which the butt is in the air, the body folded at the hips to make a right angle) to forward fold (in which the body folds as tightly as possible, like a pocket knife, feet standing together, hands alongside) is for most practitioners, an awkward jump of the feet from the back of the mat to the spot between their hands. Heather does not jump. Instead, she leans her weight into her hands, as if about to lift into handstand. For a moment her hips are high, directly over her shoulders, and her shoulders are stacked directly above her strong arms, her steady hands; her legs, straight, are folded tight to her torso, and her feet hover, weightless, a few inches above the ground. Then she places her feet, gently, seemingly effortlessly, onto the mat between her hands.

For the rest of the students, and for myself, the transitions of vinyasa clearly require effort. Alan shows off his strength but flexibility requires effort for him. Jen's injury troubles her, but it keeps her focused on breathing too: she is a better, more present, student than usual. Today's class goes well: I can hear they are breathing, which means they are paying attention to the breathing, which means they are focused and above all that is the point.

I feel good when class ends, relieved of myself and also like I have achieved some good by relieving others of themselves for a little while too. After class I ask the two new students how it went and their responses are clipped and quick, from which I gather that this class wasn't quite the right style for them. When I ask, it turns out their main experience is with Bikram yoga, which is practiced in a very hot studio and involves a different sequence with lots of sweaty balances and, in my opinion, much less overall exertion. The heat makes you sweat in Bikram; in any other vinyasa class it's the work makes you sweat, and you work very hard indeed. Much about my class must have felt peculiar, not to mention, I smugly imagine, humbling.

"Come back and try it again," I say. "It is different, but different styles of yoga can complement each other well." They nod and smile and effuse with lots of non-committal nodding, which doesn't bother me. I am in post-class glow and it's all good.

Heather lingers after class ends.

"Hey, Em" she says quietly when the room has cleared, "do you still have that friend who does the wrought iron work?"

"Tania?" I pause "Sort of. We haven't spoken in a while. I could still get you in touch with her though, I think."

I am pretty sure Heather follows my meaning: we broke up.

"Would it be awkward?" she asks.

"Nah." But it *would* be awkward. Still, I'd do it for Heather, and anyway it would be good to break the silence with Tania. I'd like to be on speaking terms, even if we can't stand to be in each other's lives any more.

"That'd be great if you could. I wonder if she'd consult with me about a storm door type of thing I want."

"I'll ask. I'll let you know later this week, OK? You in class Thursday?"

"Maybe. I'm teaching right after your class though. Hot yoga in Studio B. So I will see you."

"OK, sounds good."

Heather pauses, looking worried "Actually Em, it's OK. I can look her up myself."

"Uh" I'm fumbling. I want to do this for Heather, but I guess she's caught me out on my *faux* casualness. "OK."

"I can find her, I'm sure. I'll Google her."

I wish I still had Tania's number on my phone, but I deleted it months ago, to keep myself from calling or texting her in a weak moment: "Yeah. OK, that'll work. Her last name is Batavia, like old Dutch Indonesia."

"Ha!" jokes Heather, "Don't ask me to find that on a map! OK, I got it. Thanks, Em."

Back home there's no getting around it: I missed Will's call, and missed seeing Will. I hate that I didn't get to see him because of my aversion to the phone. I resolve to answer my phone every day, every time it rings, every single time. To just answer it. Not to wait, not to hide from whatever new problems it might want to impose on my day.

In the next days, the result of all my phone answering is that I am reminded that while some of my fellow teachers are primarily yoga teachers, like Heather and myself, most are college students who teach just a class or two a week and get overwhelmed when school kicks up. With the onset of fall, they start flaking out. I get a call from the Weinberg YMCA on thirty-third street asking if I want to pick up a kundalini class on Fridays at noon. Yes, I do: not much for recompense, but the Y is only five minutes from home by car, so it is convenient. And I get another call from the nice little hot yoga studio just off the Towson circle asking if I want to pick up a Sunday seven a.m. vinyasa class. I don't. Sundays are Alhambra walks, damn it. But that little studio is great, and I would love to teach more classes there, so it seems like being willing now might work to my advantage later. I agree, thinking that Sunday afternoons will probably still be pretty nice for an Alhambra walk.

Maple seeds, winged samara, spin in the air as they fall. Light-wind-shadows, they dance to land softly: twirl.

The white-blond boy has weathered too many storms. His not-father has been heavy-handed with the boy, striking him. The grown man is jealous, for Birdie loves her son. The man's anger germinates out of envy.

Like a tree, the pale boy's branches have been broken, and broken again, but they have healed.

His heart aches and widens into darkness.

At first, he meets the dark in him with his own quickness.

The boy's voice is warm over his small sister, chirping with light. She burbles happiness in response; she grows plump in his effervescent, dappled sunshine. His lightness is love to her and she thrives. She loves him demandingly.

It is too much then, for the boy. He can cover his own sadness with levity, but his sister wants from him the blood-weight of deep emotion, and he cannot. It is too much to ask of him: he can neither provide nor explain. Hollow- hearted. His gladwit camouflage becomes insufficient for the grey-eyed girl.

He has to withdraw.

He fills his injury with poppy flowers. Unhappy

flowers, full-bellied under their bright petals. They provide a fleeting moment of warmth, of feeling right-placed.

It is a sweet honeydew lie, the poppy and its milk of Paradise. The flower makes mean and empty the hungriest space of all, a cavity that grows and growls and yearns.

Worse than the unhappy flower is the new sap the humans themselves have made. So weightless, scentless, colorless they can soak a thin plastic leaf with it. Fentanyl, a not-flower, it brings them numb and falling down all the way to death.

The pale boy is grown. He is a winged seed that spins out and away. He is falling down.

Anyway, I did get a ticket from the city. I must have jinxed myself by thinking it could happen. It is only my second one in twenty years of the house being vacant. The yard needs to be cleaned up, they say this time, as part of the city's rat abatement efforts: "keep your grass short!" Well, the grass at Ma's is totally obscured by weeds. I amuse myself for a while contemplating the idea of contesting the ticket in court, claiming, as some folks in the nicer neighborhoods have done, that the overgrown yard is a wildlife preserve with indigenous Chesapeake flowers and plants. Then I for real decide that on Sunday I'll go down there, with Tyrell if he's free, and spend the day, likely the whole day, trying to clean up the mess.

When I ask, it turns out Tyrell isn't free Sunday. He's got to go to church with his daughter Nyasha, her kids and her new boyfriend. It's an all-day thing, and he's got to wear a suit, polish his shoes and all that. He says his daughter is going to buy him a nice hat, because everyone wears hats at her church up on Edmondson Avenue. He teased me though, about doing the yard work, brought up all the old stuff with Allidah.

"Oh, *Sir!*" Tyrell said, smirking, "I thought you didn't *do* yard work anymore!!"

"Shut *up*, Tyrell!" I grinned back at him.

The old story. It's so old now that I've finessed it for dramatic effect. An unsuspecting person might ask "Why'd you get divorced, Danny?" and I then I'll spit the whole dang thing out:

I met Allidah at Community College. I was studying accounting, and she was working in the Student Development and Careers office. She was eight years older than me, already thirty to my twenty-two. She had a full lower lip that I couldn't resist. She was bossy and confident.   I wanted all of that. We courted, dated, I bought her gifts; we got married. After BCCC, I got a job but I hated working in an accountant's office, hated wearing ties. I quit after a little less than a year and got a job driving a paint delivery truck instead, all up the Eastern cities: Philadelphia, Trenton, Pittsburgh, Ocean City. I liked being on the road seeing things. I liked all the different weather and landscapes.

Allidah hated that I was driving and lifting, hated that I was going blue collar on her. We fought about money, even though the driving and delivery money was better than what I got paid as a junior accountant and the paint delivery job came with a van that I could use evenings and weekends. We fought about kids (she wanted them, I didn't, or at least not then). Though it all really was about the bigger things like money and kids, on the surface of it we fought most about the yard.

We bought a little row house on Oakland Ave., over in Wilson Park. It was walking distance to Ma's house, though Allidah would hardly ever walk over there with me because, she claimed, I was just too weird afterwards. Ma died of cancer after we'd been in Wilson Park just a couple of years.

Anyway, Oakland Ave. was quiet. Tiny yards front and back. They were so small, it never seemed worth the trouble to mow, so I let the grass go to seed and the sweet white virgin's bower climb all on the chain link fence. I liked the green, I liked the flowers. I liked the grass when it went to seed like wheat. I even liked the bright yellow dandelion flowers. Altogether, I thought an overgrown front and back yard was a pleasing addition. What would we have done with those tiny spaces anyway? Gotten a tiny dog perhaps, to poop tiny poops in them?

Allidah thought the grass should be clipped low. She thought the overgrowth provided a place for potential muggers or drug dealers to hide: clean chain link would be better. No one can hide in chain link. In addition, she insisted the mowing was a man's job, my job. Her job was to chide me about the mowing. My *not* mowing became the focus of her discontents. She'd cross her angry arms over her chest, and that lovely lower lip of hers would go hard and wrinkled like a dead worm. By our fifth anniversary our relationship was pretty cold.

I met someone else, a nice young woman who lived with *her* elderly mother clear over the other side of town, near Druid Hill. Oh, she was sweet. Both her lips were plump and soft, though she never let me kiss her. My dick'd go hard the instant she smiled at me, like an air traffic control flag pointing me, the whole damn jet, in her direction. I'd be torn between trying to follow my dang dick and trying to hide the gesture it was making towards her. She teased me and flirted but she knew I was a married man. She knew I wanted her real bad, but she never, not once, slept with me, in spite of all my efforts to charm her.

One of my charms was offering to mow her lawn. It was the most chivalrous thing I could think to do. I put the mower in the van on a weekend delivery run and drove to her house after I'd done work. I didn't think Allidah noticed my rolling the mower out of the shed in back. But of course, she thought it was very suspicious that I'd touched the mower at all. I guess I could have thought of that. Allidah followed me. She must have followed me all day. That day I drove into DC and back. I wasn't watching for anyone following. Maybe if I had been, I would have seen her car. She must have been really careful, and so patient. She followed me for the whole trip, and then hid around the corner when I pulled up late afternoon to do the sweet girl's lawn.

I was tired, cheerful, and inexperienced. I had to wrangle awkwardly with the orange electric cord. There was an embarrassing moment when I had to remember how the thing turned on. The girl laughed at me, and with me. Her lawn was small too, like mine, but shady with a view of Druid Hill's trees and the curving road leading to the zoo not too far off. She was smiling on her porch, bringing me a glass of Gatorade, when Allidah finally decided to reveal herself. She pulled her little brown Honda up in front of the house and I felt the air go cold all round me.

"What the *hell* are you doing, Danny?" Allidah yelled though her passenger window, as she leaned across the front seat to roll it down. "What the *hell*? You can't do our lawn, but you can do this hussy bitch's yard? What the *hell*?"

She drove off without waiting for my response, and by the time I got home she had packed a suitcase. She sat in the living room lounge chair, arms crossed over her bosom, lips hard, as I walked sheepishly in the back door. From the suitcase, I thought *she* was leaving, but no. She'd packed a suitcase for *me*. Dirty laundry out of the hamper, it turned out to be, and filthy workboots in a plastic bag with my toothbrush. She wouldn't believe there hadn't been an affair, and anyway she didn't care one way or the other.

"Mowing that woman's lawn. Yuh-huh. Sounds like it *is* what it was! I *bet* you enjoyed her lawn alright," she said.

Mowing, thick with innuendo, was the end of my marriage. Sweet girl never slept with me either, because I'd proven myself a bad person, courting her while married.

Of course, Tyrell knows all this. He heard the story right after it happened because I went to stay with him, in his multi-generational and crowded house, when Allidah kicked me out. He heard me polish and refine the yarn for laughs as time went by. It's a joke between us still, because he borrows my mower, and I don't date: "I might as well borrow it!" he'll jab. "You never mow nothing no more."

Come Sunday I get up at ten, which is early for me. I make tea, and put some in a jar to drink later. I put the tea and some hedge trimmers in my old back pack, balance the weed whacker on my shoulder and with my other hand push the lawn mower down the side walk. Pushing the mower while balancing the whacker makes for a walk that feels long. It seems the city has ripped up and patched almost every part of the pavement along my route, trying, unsuccessfully, to stop leaks in the elderly water mains underground. So there's bumpy pavement for the hard lawnmower wheels to clatter over, and in spite of it all, I can see a new spot of tarmac that's seeping water right in the middle of Alhambra, just a short ways down the slope from Ma's.

I haven't even done any work yet, but when I get to Ma's I stop and rest for a while on the steps up from the side walk to the house. I wish I'd brought something to eat. I don't usually eat breakfast, but I'm hungry before I even start.

There's so much to do; it seems so unlikely I'll be able to beat back the wall of green. One small human against the huge energy of growing plants; it seems futile to even try. I decide to begin in the back, where the yard slopes less. I start, right in the center of the back lawn, to hack down to a foot or so of growth with the hedge trimmers. I plan, I hope, that the lawnmower might be able to bulldoze the stuff once I've got it that short.

It's fine once I get started. Leveling everything down becomes a kind of compulsion.   It's easy to focus. I feel self-conscious though, aware of how inept my clipping might look given how much overgrowth there is. But who's watching? The plants? I work outwards, making a circle of shorter greenery. To amuse myself, I imagine it as a miniature coliseum from which the on-looking plants can cheer on their kind and watch for my demise. The cut green smells good. Though manual not electric, the hedge trimmers are sharp enough to get through the saplings and vines. Bending over for so long is tough on the low back though. I've got to stand up to stretch every ten minutes or so.

I've been at it for about an hour, long enough for the sweat to be running down my spine like a stream, and for the circle of shorter growth, the coliseum, to be big enough maybe for a Roman tiger to pace around in, when a vine gets really caught, mangled and sticky, in the trimmer's blades. I stop, still hunched over, and start working the macerated fibers free, loosening things back up.

From where I am, I can see between the bushes along the side of the house, but it takes me a moment to realize that someone is standing out on the sidewalk. I wouldn't really have noticed, except for the two dogs—big and little—fidgeting, snuffling and pulling to the edge of the circles of movement their leashes permit. It's Em and her dogs. She's got her hand up to her forehead to keep the sun off her eyes, and she's looking up at Ma's house.

What on earth? She stands just like that for a long time. I try to imagine what she's seeing there. The upstairs windows aren't boarded up, but it's dark in the house. It's not like she can see in. Maybe there's a squirrel on the roof doing something interesting? But why is she *here*, looking at *this house*, Ma's house?

I stand up and glare at her through my sunglasses, planning to be mad.

She startles, pivots slightly to find the movement, and sees it's me.

Her face! So ridiculous the anger leaves me. All expression, all muscle, all wrinkle and line, fall flat out of it and her mouth hangs open for a few seconds. Then, as Ma would say, "quick like a bunny," she snatches the leashes in her palms up high in front of her chest and tries to bolt. The dogs don't care to move so quick as her though, and she's struggling, trying to run away while they want to keep dawdling. She's got her head down, back round, shoulders up, as if I am going to throw something at her as she goes. The leashes are tangled in front of her. The little dog is keening towards me, tail wagging. Em's tripping and stumbling but continuing to try and run away. She's more like the tortoise than the hare trying to sprint. I start to laugh, and to push through the plants around the side of the house to keep sight of her.

It's just before noon, the sun bright overhead, when I turn down Alhambra with Girlfriend and Blue. I've stopped on the sidewalk outside the peeling blue house, and am shielding my eyes from the sun. I look up for a good long while, admiring the tall peak of the roof, the pretty upstairs windows. Then something in the back yard moves. I startle. It's Danny, standing up from a crouching position in the back of the garden.

Shit! What's he doing here? He's never here. Why's he in the back yard? Maybe he didn't see me? I am embarrassed and adrenaline sparks in me: I spin around and yank the dogs abruptly back down Alhambra.

"Em!" He calls out. "Hey Em, whatcha doing?" There's a laugh from him as I keep walking, head down, mortified. I can hear him rustling through the overgrowth as he struggles towards the front yard, "Em! Honey, I can *see* you." He's chuckling; I am almost running.

Then I hear him fall. I hear the crunches of branches and green leaves, I hear a big crash like a surge of water, and then there's quiet. I pivot again, confused but delighted dogs panting and tangling their leather leashes, and start to run back to the house and up the steps.

"Danny? Where are you Danny?" Blue starts to bark.

Girlfriend is so tangled in his leash that his barks jerk her closer to him. "Danny?"

"I'm here. I'm OK." The voice comes from the side of the house.

Jesus. I hope this stuff isn't actually all poison ivy. I push through the plants, hauling the dogs behind me. Blue stops barking because I'm pulling him neck first into bushes. He's got his head twisted to the side to avoid the worst of it. Girlfriend surges forward through the softer, small plants low down. She gets to Danny first, wagging and clucking, triumphant even, the picture of a happy hound arriving at the source of a scent trail, like *she's* found Danny and wants to point him out to me. I haul her back so she doesn't stand on him. He's on his hands and knees in some of the bigger thornier bushes, plants that look, closer up, to once have been roses. He's trying to stand up and failing. At first I think he's hurt himself badly: there's some blood on his hands and his face. Then I realize he's struggling to stand because he's laughing so hard. He can't breathe he's laughing so much.

"Jesus, Danny. C'mon." I am angry, embarrassed, and worried all at once. I lean down to grab his upper arm, Girlfriend lunges toward him in the same moment and I stumble a bit: one of the rose branches prangs my forehead. "Ouch. Fuck!" Blue starts barking again.

"*You* OK, Em?" yells Danny over the barking, trying to look up.

"Yeah. *Blue!* Shut up, dog!" I bend again for Danny's arm, grab it and help him to stand. He's still shuddering with giggles as he pushes his sunglasses back up his nose, and rights his hat.

"Your nose is bleeding." I say.

"Yeah," he says, wiping it and looking at the back of his hand where the blood has smeared.

"Your hands too." He looks at the palms, slightly more scraped on the right than on the left. The left one is basically fine.

"Hey Em," he says looking at me. "You are bleeding too! Your head."

I wipe my forehead with the back of my free arm, the one not holding the excited, squirming dogs on their leashes, and there is blood there. Not much though.

When she's wiped the blood off a bit I see where the thorns got her. Right between her eyebrows. Two small, bloody dots. I stop laughing.

"What are you doing here, Em?"

Things root when they are distracted, pleased, lightened in spite of themselves.

People, plants: they grow when they can stretch through or around their injuries in search of new lightness—laughter, sunshine, altitude.

Roots can only go down dark deep, digest, embrace the soil, if there is delight to grow green up towards.

Sometimes I have to surprise with lightness or there can be no resolving the darkness into its place.

Over the lives, I have done it sometimes.

Once, Summer:

She was one of Walters's Percherons, a tall mare, grey and white dapples broad on her strong flanks like the water where it swirls in a river cataract, white frothing up strong and circular around dark slate. She loved the man with the dusty dark hands. She liked to rub her long white forehead up and down the length of his chest, that shirt that smells faintly of sheep. She rubbed hard, pushed, nearly knocking him over. With strong hands, one on each side of her neck, he clapped her, loudly, laughing. She shook her head, leaving short white hairs in the air between them, whinnied, curling her upper lip and showing her happiness.

The man's daughter was a puppy-child yipping in

the yard, weaving little mats and dolls out of the straw, letting the mare nibble her hair where it was twisted up in fluffs like dandelion plumes on short thick stems. When the girl died—an accident with a fire, and burnt skin, painful injury, a doctor sent for and yelling—the man with the duststrong hands stood in the dark of the mare's stall, in the pee-damp corner where it is most dark, and he cried.

For somelongtime seasons, even if the horse nibbled his buttons, the furze of his hair, he wouldn't laugh.

Then the horses were sold off, bit by bit, fewer of them each week, the yard echoing with fewer hoof-falls. The farrier, big red arms pressing pasterns into his long leather apron, hot metals, the smell of singed hoof, spent less time banging his anvil.

She, the lovely Percheron mare, had to go into the ring, the auction ring, and there were men's faces and voices thick around it like bushes rustling with wind. A pink round loud man with a small wooden hammer was yelling fast while the stable man, with his darkstrong hands, hung his head to the white railing and would not look at his horse. She felt her hide pucker and shiver. She didn't want the man to leave her in the ring. She threw her tail up, her hooves. She couldn't see right.

Then the earth tumbled, I tumbled. The wind, my wind, blew stones and sand in the air. The horse couldn't see. She fell. I rose to her, knocked her hard, bloodied her knees. Sand in the air: she was blind. She lay in the dirt. I held her down. She couldn't get up from me. It came silent.

"No bidders? No bidders!" the round man yelled. "Who'll take her for a penny?" There was laughter. "Penny for some dog food, gentlemen! Don't know how you'll get her home though! Have to shoot her and drag her, I reckon." They let their dogs in to chase the horse, making to rouse her. She couldn't see. Then the man, the darkstrong hands man: "Sir."

There was jeering, but after, after all, as the light drained from the afternoon and the sharp acrid shit smell dulled, she could stand again. I let her go. The mare snuffled the man's hands. He brought her water.

Arabbers. What they call the horse carts, the small horses that pull them. She was taller than all of them. They took shelter with the arabbers. The man got bright fabric for his horse's bridle, and bells too. She pulled a cart, a light cart, just vegetables and fruits: easy. She would jingle the bells by shaking her head, and curl her top lip to the sky and her man would laugh. He laughed again. All the sun long, it was running, it was lovely.

Another Time, It Was Winter, A Long Winter:
He was a pigtown man, a bacon and lard man, his home a retreat in the sweet air of buttercup and chicory, yellow and blue, hills and valleys off and east of the York Road. Thomas Cassard came home with the smell of pig shit still on his clothes. His discontents ran deeper even

than the smells on his skin, down to his selfsame core: even amidst the fragrant flowers of his verdant retreat, he dreamt of France. He named the lanes that ran down my hill to the stream Beaumont and Chateau. Thomas had a wife, pale Mina with dark eyes like a deer's eyes at night when the moonlight catches the pooled water in them. Mina wanted the babies that died within her. Over and over they wrenched themselves free of her, tiny and white with their round heads driving down, fingers and toes like the splayed digits of a lizard. It was a continually renewing tragedy, the sound of the woman's grieved crying. So much blood pooling into white sheets that were then burnt outside, their ash to seep into my soil. Tiny babies interred beneath the ivy and black walnut trees, their souls leaching down, headed for the Chesapeake.

He raged when she died, the sheets red around her, blood running through the mattress to drip onto the wood floor and between those boards into my soil beneath. He railed at the sky, knelt in the snow outside his house and cursed everything, most especially children.

But the slope of snow between Beaumont and Chateau was bright and glittered. It was tempting, the light in the crystalline ice. It was a perfect playground, a sweep and flank of my land perfect for such childish delights as sledding. In the bright cold months after, children swarmed over and under his fence with planks of wood and pieces of tin to sled raucously down the hill. He yelled at them to get off his land, tears standing in his red-rimmed eyes. They responded:

Cass-ard, Cass-ard, can only sell lard.

Wants to speak French, but it is too hard!

He yelled more. Then, to make him happy too, as happy as the naughty delighted children with their exhilarated breaths steaming my air, I let some of them slide too fast, my snowy hill icy with repeated use, and they hurtled out of control past the boulders at the bottom and straight into my frigid stream where they yowled and yelled before scrambling out, steely water pouring out the sides of their laced leather boots, and scurried home while Cassard laughed and laughed. He too laughed.

Or, Time At Night:

Not a tree. It is upside down, as though a crown of branches and leaves may be underground. It has its roots in the sky. Metal trunk, metal roots, each ending in a bell. Together the bells should ring the hour. The Curran clock. Memorial: it is the clock they made to remember when a man's heart stopped beating, when he was scared to death.

Funny place to put it, here, this soil, Woodbourne and York, not in the city spot where the man's wits jumped from him in fear as gunshot left smoke in the air all round. Look up through the roots. Look up through the underside and you can see the stars pricking the sky with light, marking time. Look up through the roosting bells in these roots to see bolt-light slicing down, cacophonous with a smell like gunshot. I send lightning to those roots. The clock time stops at midnight. Star time begins.

They replace it: the metal tree is logged and milled away, a demure green clocktower is put in its place, ugly human green like no plant. A white clock face in front of a littered parking lot in front of a boarded-up grocery store. Nothing here gives life. A man pees in the bus shelter in the dark, long after the traffic has stilled. His friend waits alongside, looking down at the ugliness around.

The new clock does not even have roots.

Lightning to the new clock. Bolt-light slice bang again.

In the darkness, two men cringe at the shock if it, the surprise, the sudden axe-split noise.

Their mouths hang open and the tang of electric smoke tickles the backs of their alcohol-dry tongues.

"This the new clock?"

"Y'uh huh."

"Because the other one was broke?"

"Yessir."

"Couldn't tell no time?"

"You bet."

"And this's the new one?"

The hands on the clock face are tidily together, stilled here again with long and short both heading direct up to the stars, again, to star time once more.

The men start laughing, slapping each other on the back, slapping their own bony knees, laughing and laughing until the hope left deep and hidden in the lungs of them has swirled out into the air and they are buoyed up by it a little, by the aspirant joy of it.

And This:

My rose bushes next to the house in which the girl fell and then later died. My rose bushes. The dogwalker and the thin man, and my thorns on rose bushes. By calling the dogwalker here, by shocking her, I made the thin man laugh. Also, my rose thorns marked her brow, showed him his fallen sister's face. Laughter first, and then I let them see more clearly. I have water flowing underground, juices seeping, ready to make lightness burst up.

Commingle the lightness and the work.
It is not easy to grow. It hurts them, growing.
Lightness first, but then they must.

IT IS SHIFTING NOW
DANNY-EM

It goes back and forth between the dogwalker and the thin man, back and forth, the thing they feel but can't think through. Wind through my leaves; the silver undersides turn up like a storm is coming.

Em's face has gone all slack again, still and flat. I can't stop looking at the two little dots of blood, just so, exactly in the spot where Linnie had her umlaut.

"What are you doing here?"

Her face is still, but her eyes are searching me, my face.

It is a struggle: the two of us are squabbling over this overgrown plot, like squirrels fighting over territory. She's looking at me.

I am looking at Danny and Jesus God Almighty. I can't think of a thing to say. Why am I here? I don't know. I have to be here. I want to be here. I feel like I just need to be at this house. But what can I possibly tell him? It doesn't make sense to me either. So I lead with apology, and deflection:

"Uh. I'm sorry. Are you OK? Your nose is still

bleeding." I root in my pockets for a kleenex and come up only with a plastic bag for dog poop scooping.

"Em, Miss Em, I am *fine*. But tell me, what are you doing looking at my house?"

"Your Mother's house."

There's a moment that the wind blows through and both look up to see the undersides of the leaves, silver where they are blown. She looks back to Danny, sees him furious, his mouth working silent shapes. He's staring at her, fierce behind his sunglasses, shoulders lifting as he gets ready to launch his words.

I can't believe that girl! The nerve. It *is* my house, Ma is long dead. I glare at Em.

"It is my house now. Why are you here, Em?" I am stern, angry. Her face tightens up. I can hear her sharp inhale as she steps awkwardly back from me.

Trying to back away from him in the closed world of greenery, inside these noisy bushes, she can smell the hammy warmth of his breath as the wind catches it. She spits back:

"Just walking, Danny, *Mister* Danny. The dogs like to walk down here. Nice and shady. Thought maybe they could shit in your yard as it's such a mess anyway you wouldn't mind."

He's mad. I am confused. I am physically uncomfortable. We are standing too close together, forced into proximity in the bushes. My impulses conflict: I want to help him wipe up his bleeding nose, but he's so mad I also just want to get away. He wants me to go away.

"I'll be off now, if you don't need my help," I say to Danny as he turns so I am talking to the back of his shoulder.

Turning to face into the wind, I am dismissing her, that woman and her dogs. Over my shoulder I croon, jasmine-flower sweet "Fine, Miss Em, that's fine. You all have a *nice* day now, you hear?" I am beyond annoyed: I am livid, angrier than I've been in years. I've got my back mostly to her. "Bye bye now," I say, waving over my shoulder, my hand cupped a little, a rotation of the hand at the wrist like the Queen of England waving at a parade. I mean it, the words and the gesture both, sarcastically. It's me giving her the finger.

Back and forth.

Time to slow them through what has been unsettled.

Here are the silvered undersides of their own leaves in the wind: storm coming.

Em

He just dismisses me, angry, and turns his back. I shake my hands out towards him, flipping him off with both middle fingers, dog leashes dangling over my forearm for a moment, unsecured. I sneer. I can feel my upper lip curl far up on the right side, an impotent adolescent face. Then I exhale sharply. *What the fuck.* I carefully re-grasp the leashes, look for the route I took into the bushes to help me get my way back out.

On Alhambra, I walk right down the middle of the road, which is patched and lumpy, with a big puddle at the bottom of the valley, water welling up from some broken water main. I am preoccupied with Danny, not paying attention, and walk right into the water, getting my blundstones thoroughly wet, Girlfriend and Blue straining to the sides: hound dogs don't like to get their feet wet. It's just one more stupid thing I have done today, one more way to feel like an idiot. The water that splashes on my calves makes them itch. I lean down to see a rash, an already livid braille, spangling my calves and thighs: poison ivy. The puddle also makes the insoles of my boots so wet they wheeze as I walk, squelching out water and air with every noisy footfall.

The whole squelching walk home, and all the rest of that infernally itchy day, I have conversations in my head, variations in which I don't try and run away after being seen and in which I answer Danny's question "What are you doing here, Em?" better. I rehearse different responses and trace all the better ways the conversation could have gone: I am birdwatching, I am looking for you (that's a good one! But why am I looking for him?), I am interested in gables, I just love old houses. I puzzle over answers. I know my mock-up conversations are implausible but they all end with another fantastical, impossible thing I want for inexplicable reasons: Danny offering to show me inside the house. Clearly that's not going to happen, not after today.

Danny

Dang it. Dang Dang Dang. After my thing with Em, I am just upset. The circular coliseum I've made in the grass looks ridiculous, like a bad crop circle. I get the clippers unstuck and swipe savagely into the brush growth, venting my anger. I clear messy swaths now, no shape to them, I just clear and clear. I guess I am hungry. My stomach feels sour and burning though. When I stand up to straighten my back, I feel light headed.

It must be mid-afternoon when I stop, daunted by suddenly remembering that on the walk back up the hill to my house I will have to push the mower and carry the weedwhacker. I haven't even used them yet. Realizing that if carrying them home sounds like too much work right now, like I just can't do it, don't have the energy, then revving them up is probably a bad idea. I don't need to run over my foot with the mower today, or weedwhack my shins: better to rest a moment and then take the walk home with all the stuff I haven't used even if I am not done. I survey the back yard: you can walk across it now, at least. It's not short like mown grass, but it is clearly a yard. It's something.

I head round to the front with the clippers, mower and whacker, dumping them and my old bag on the sidewalk before sitting down on the bottommost of the front steps. It takes me a long time to remember I have a jar of tea. Left to sit for so long, it is neither cool nor hot: it's the same temperature as the inside of my cheeks. I can barely feel it's there when I take a sip. On my sour tongue, it tastes like metal. I sit with my back to the house, shoulders hunched, sipping. Like Em with her shoulders up running from me, I must look like some kind of turtle, shell on its back to protect itself. I am still so angry. I can't look at the stupid house.

Across the street a woman—short cropped grey hair, drooping pouches under her eyes—comes out of her house. She's wearing a white undershirt over saggy breasts and big khaki shorts. She's got her cigarette and lighter out and goes to sit on her porch, sees me, raises her palm in greeting, but then shuffles off round the side to where an old SUV is parked, where I can't see her. I feel like I should know who she is, like she knows me but I can't remember her. I don't know who lives in that house now. It's been too long.

I feel *upset*.

Upset is the right word: knocked over, thrown off. I saw Linnie's umlaut, right here, right by the house, on Em I am so angry I could punch something, or cry.

The walk home is miserable. I've lost the knack of balancing the weedwhacker on my shoulder; it keeps slipping off and I keep having to stop to adjust it. The bumpy road seems to stop the lawnmower every few feet, jarring me and making it impossible to keep up any momentum. Turning off Alhambra, the hill up to York is steep. I'm tired and hungry even though my stomach now burns painfully. It's gotten surprisingly hot but I can't sweat anymore. When I finally get to my own front steps, I throw the whacker up onto the porch, not really caring if the dang thing breaks (though even as I do it I regret the possibility of it breaking: I can't afford to replace it right now). I haul the lawnmower up the steps behind me. Inelegant. There's no strength left in me. I leave the two contraptions sprawled in the middle of my porch. They look like they've collapsed there, which is just how I feel.

I go in to drink some water, filling a glass at the sink. I decide I'll eat some applesauce. I have some single serve pots of it in the fridge, from Giant's "Back to School" sale. I don't ordinarily eat applesauce, but six little pots for forty-five cents seemed like a great deal. It should be nice and cold, and should soothe my sore stomach. Em's dang Coors is still in the fridge too. It makes me angry all over again.

I look in the drawer for my favorite spoon. It's an old piece of airline cutlery, from the era when even "tourist class" seating involved a meal, and that meal involved linens and cutlery. That era happened to also be the era when I flew every year as an unaccompanied minor from air force bases back to Baltimore. The spoon's from Singapore Airlines. That was always one of the best airlines to fly, with the pretty stewardesses in their batik uniforms. The spoon's head is like a rectangle with rounded corners and a shallow bowl. It's on the small side, closer to a teaspoon really. I see it in the drawer, grab it and then fumble with hands still stiff and numb from too much yard clipping. Clumsy, I tick the spoon abruptly against the counter top which sends it spinning sideways. I watch it spin, clutch for it, and inadvertently hit rather than catch it so it ricochets further along the counter to fall down in the narrow space between the counter and my gas stove.

Shiiiit. Motherfucker Shit. I don't normally swear, but this is just the last *fucking* straw. A whole miserable day and now my spoon, my favorite relic of another time, another me, is lost in the dark space I can't reach between counter and stove. It is a GAS stove, which means there's no unplugging it and shimmying it out to get the spoon. *Dang. Damn. Fuck.* I put the unopened apple sauce back in the fridge and go into the living room to lie down on the couch. I sprawl on it, face first, but that reminds me, with a surprise like being slapped, of the day when I was seven and on my way to change Linnie's diaper and lay down on the couch instead. *Damn it.* I get up to go take a shower.

Of course Em has no idea, and the marks on her forehead are just an accident, just the overgrown bushes talking. I still want to blame her, somehow, for them, or maybe blame the bushes. I don't know. I want to blame someone, something. I am trying to settle down but I still can't shake my desire to yell at Em, or cry, or thrash about: I need some way to shake the fire in my nerves.

I'd had the bathtub ripped out before I even moved into this place. Upstairs now it is just a shower, glass walls and a sliding door. A nice big square. Bright, modern, great adjustable shower head. I hate bathtubs. The shower is good. I let the water be cold, let it send its sharpness down to my aching head. It feels good.

After, I dress in clean clothes, go get a glass of iced tea, long since bitter from being in the pot all day, and sit outside on the porch, in the dark, watching the cars go by. I think of little Linnie's face. Her sweet cheeks. Her birthmark. How I've always missed her. Linnie. Little Linnie. Poor Linnie. I remember her as perfect Linnie, not damaged Linnie. I remember her before the fall, blocking out the drooling and staring eyes. I remember her as sweet Linnie, good enough to eat. I remember making her squeal by pretending to eat her fat little thighs.

The morning is hot and humid. My early dogwalk (Saturday morning tulip garden) is sweaty enough that I take a shower and change clothes after it. No classes this morning, nothing until tomorrow's early vinyasa session in Towson, so after toast and tea I lie down on the couch in the old rumpus room, what I refer to now as my lounge, and fall asleep.

Thunder, and Blue's panting, wake me out of a dream, to rain pelting hard against window glass. The windows are all shut, thankfully. Though the storm is breaking up the humid air, washing in some coolness, the early morning had been unseasonably, almost malevolently, hot and clammy. I was running the central air (installed expensively when Mother renovated; she was extra smug about it because none of the neighbors had central air yet).

There is an abrupt and loud splitting of the heavens seemingly directly overhead—thunder. Blue's panting and shivering next to the couch intensifies. He is crouched low as if he is trying to get under both me and the furniture. Girlfriend, unfazed, is sleeping next to the TV, with her favorite nylabone nestled under her nose.

I feel disoriented, waking into such violent weather, and waking from a deep sleep at the wrong time of day. The rain comes down in gouts, fast and heavy. I can't see the lightning but every two or three minutes there is another resounding explosion of thunder, close overhead and loud. I sit up, and Blue leaps onto the couch, pressing up close, shaking and panting. I reassure him, hugging him hard around his big rib cage, then I get up. I shut off the ac, and move to look out the kitchen window. I watch the thick grey rain.

What a week for dreams! One familiar one that repeats (I think of this one now as 'the spinning dream'), and now this nap offered me two peculiar new ones. In total then, there are three weird dreams, all detailed, each unnerving.

Since last Sunday, and quarreling with Danny on Alhambra by his Ma's house, I've had the spinning dream every night. It starts with blue and yellow light on a black and white tile floor. Then I am spinning, and I see the room in the dream is a bathroom, with an old white enamel tub. Then I can see into the mirror over the sink. The sink is old too, two slightly rusty taps, not one; it is stained white porcelain with two metal supporting legs at the front, no cabinet underneath, no counter. The mirror above the sink is foxed at the edges. The face I see in it is a black woman's face, her eyes closed. Wrinkles branch from the outside corners of her closed eyes. There's a furrow in the middle of her forehead: it makes her look worried. Her hair is tied up in a plain, pale headscarf. Her face looks tired. From the angle of her shoulders and her arms I can see she's holding on to the edges of the sink. There's the sound of water dripping. Then I start spinning again, and then I see the green and gold light on the tile floor. It's always the same. I feel sick to my stomach when I wake, like I have motion sickness.

In the first of my new stormy naptime dreams, I still feel I am myself, but when I catch glimpses of my body I have dark brown skin. I am myself but also a black child, a black *boy*. I am in the same bathroom, but I have a different perspective. I stand to one side of the tub. I am not tall enough to see in the mirror. I am eye-level with the middle of the woman's back as she clutches the sink. I can see that she is wearing a white T-shirt tucked into a knee-length light cotton skirt that has a pattern on it, reddish, maybe flowers. The dripping from the tub's faucet is in this dream too. I can see there's a semicircular stained glass window, high up, with some kind of bird. It filters the sunlight green, gold and blue on the tiles of the floor. I look up at the window. I am terrified.

The second new dream takes place outside, at night. It is high up. There are dozens of crows roosting in an oak tree, their silhouettes darker than the night sky. The big dark birds are eerily silent. There's a rooftop, nearby. In the diffuse light of cloudy darkness a squirrel digs to bury an acorn, except it's digging on the roof, not the ground, trying to dig a hole into sticky black asphalt roof tiles. It's digging in the steep gable roof above an attic window, like it's trying to get into the attic itself. The dream's rhythmic scrabbling becomes persistent and annoying. The squirrel's frantic dream digging synchronizes with Blue's real world raspy frightened panting, so that when I wake into my lounge it seems as if the squirrel is still digging.

Time for more tea, and maybe after that a walk, if the rain has stopped. I need to bring myself back to myself. In the kitchen, I put water on to boil. I locate my afternoon tea mug in the cupboard (morning tea gets a different mug, this one is just for later). It's a hideous thing, a gift from my mother on my fifteenth birthday that has survived the decades by never moving far from its spot in the corner of the second shelf of the cabinets to the left of the kitchen sink. It is large and egg-shaped, white ceramic with overlapping love hearts in pink, red and crimson. I have never liked the way it looks and yet the smoothness of the ceramic makes a nice cup of tea if one is brewing a tea bag in a cup—as I tend to in the afternoon—rather than in a pot which is more typical for me in the mornings. I reach up to grab the cup by its handle and, still inept from daytime sleep and strange dreams, take it too loosely, lifting the cup but not stopping the oblong weight of it from slipping down between my fingers to fall, hitting the edge of the cream-tiled countertop. I see it break against the counter before it continues falling to hit the linoleum, breaking there into even more pieces.

I am shocked that it could break after all these years.

I stand looking at the cup on the floor: really it is three large pieces and some shards. Even as some part of my brain is suggesting I could glue it back together, a swift geyser of petulant fury rises in me, and I level a swift kick at the debris so that one piece skitters across the kitchen to smack with an unsatisfyingly soft *tink* into the wall. Even my fury gets me nowhere, lame. I see myself for a moment: ridiculous. Who the hell am I? Some sort of dreamer savant? Haunted by what exactly? Why can't I just live a life, a better, fuller life? I'm a yoga teacher who doesn't believe the hype. A middle-aged frumpy white woman managing an uncomfortably mediocre existence. To what end? Not fulfilling my potential, the career office at Dickinson would say. Aptitudes according to those tests I took as a junior? National Parks Forester, Psychiatrist. Those were hilarious, improbable. Yet here I am, stagnant. I am not impressed with myself. The moment of self-mockery, the potential for hilarity, passes. All that's left is sighing, leaving me exhausted in the mess of broken ceramic.

I clean up the pieces so the dogs don't eat them, and then I don't know what to do with myself.

I don't want tea anymore. I wish I did have a yoga class to teach today, or plans to meet Bev for coffee or something. I contemplate calling her, but I don't feel like talking, and certainly not on the phone. Maybe I should get in touch with Tania, just in case Heather couldn't find her? That is such a spectacularly bad idea that I drop it immediately. It would best, perhaps, in this frame of mind, if I stop having ideas. I leave the kitchen to stand in the front entryway, watching until the rain stops. Then I get the dogs ready, and we go out to walk.

Though walks of course happen in public, I consider them private time, not social time. Maybe I'm deluding myself, but I figure if I am walking with purpose (I Am Walking The Dogs), I am invisible to the world, or irrelevant to it: not worth noticing. It's an inconvenience to encounter someone I know, to be obliged to chat if I am not expecting it.

Today, to avoid seeing Danny, I strike off west along Coldspring, away from York Road, towards Loyola. The dogs both poop on the sopping wet grass verge between the busy street and a mansion in need of repair. I don't scoop. I am starting to feel better, more myself. I pick up pace. I am watching the puddles on sidewalk, how they reflect the overhanging tree branches, not the vista ahead. I am consequently completely taken by surprise when I do look up and see, coming east on the Coldspring sidewalk, Danny. For a moment I think I am imagining things, conjuring up my least desired scenario in a kind of dream-state fug left over from my weird nap. By the time I see him it is too late to turn, to veer, to try and disappear. He's seen me. I've seen him. We walk until we are close enough to talk, and then both of us stop. He greets the dogs first, formally.

"Hey, Mr. Blue, Mizz Girlfriend," leaning down to scratch their shoulders, "Em."

"Hi Danny. How's it going?" I am deadpan. Numb. Lifeless. This day has already been so strange with dreams and tantrum that this unexpected encounter doesn't even make my blood rush to my face.

"Good. Ah. Yup. Good. Got rained on a bit in the storm. Walked over to Mom's to buy tea!" He holds up a rain-spattered paper carry bag emblazoned with "My Organic Market" as a kind of proof.

"Oh. Yeah. You make good tea with that stuff."

There's a pause. He squats down to pet the dogs again: both seem happy to see him. It's not really awkward, but neither of us says anything.

I don't blurt it, I say it slow and clear, but I wasn't planning on it. I *would* have been embarrassed if I had thought ahead:

"I'd love to see inside your Ma's house." I am shocked at myself. Danny looks astounded too. I really couldn't have said this if I wasn't in such a strange mood already. There is a long pause. Danny sucks his teeth and makes "tseh" sound. He is looking at the dogs not me as he responds.

"Yeah. OK. When?"

"Tomorrow afternoon?" Another Sunday. Seems about right. Alhambra-house Sundays.

Danny sounds resigned, like he's submitting to something outside his control.

"Sure thing, Em. Two?"

"Yeah! OK." I am feeling the awkwardness now. Now I am hearing my blood speed in my ears. Jesus! What the fuck am I doing? "Should I knock on your door? We could walk over together."

"Sounds fine. I'll see you then?"

"Yep."

He starts walking, swiftly, in the direction of York and his house, raising his free hand, the one without the grocery bag, in a wave as he goes. It's like a calmed echo of his angry wave over his shoulder in the bushes: still irritated, but not livid.

Over his shoulder he calls "Tomorrow."

"Yep" I respond as I lean to scratch the stubborn poison ivy rash that's still mottling my legs.

They have laid their soles upon me for so long.

The tallest ones, times long ago in seasons far back, had shining dark hair. All the summers long their feet were bare on the mica sparkling between the pines, the walnuts and the oaks. Those tall Susquehannocks walked the length of my spine, the central passage of what I am, single file, season after season. Frequently there would be conflict with others, battles with rocks thrown, spears, hands, arms, bone daggers, rocks rocks rocks and stones, over who was right to be walking here. Blood seeped into my soil tinting it deeper red, black. The tall ones, Susquehannocks, won in their conflicts against Haudenosaunee from afar.

In later times, these tall ones came from their homes far north and walked along here, south all the way to the Bay carrying heavy loads of beaver pelt to trade with Dutch, Swedish and English ships. The English traded clothes, blankets, beads, guns and secretly also European diseases that left the tall ones huddled in makeshift camps along my river, cold inside with a fever that forced itself out of them in sores that oozed pus and blood. They moaned on the banks of my stream, in the shelters they made of branches and their new English wool blankets. They moaned into my soil until they died and gradually washed back into the ground with the rains, the wind, and the mischief wreaked by animals—coyotes, groundhogs, bears. They were bones scattered between the rocks and trees.

The English wanted to settle over me; they wanted to cast England's valleys green like a blanket over my wild. They dragged long two-handled saws back and forth across tree trunks, dug stumps out of my heavy earth and grey rock out of my hills. They built houses and farmed. They walked, rode horses, and drew rickety carts north and north. Then they'd come south again, back down the length of me because, like the perishing Susquehannocks, they too needed to trade at the Bay. They rolled wooden hogsheads of tobacco down the length of my spine, heading to the shore for shipment away. For some long lives, my spine was known to them as Britain's Ridge Rolling Road. With the English settlers came other lives from another kind of far away, people whose skin was dark, and whose exhausted feet bore the memory of soil red with iron, of heat, of the shade of teak and baobab trees. These lives were not free. These people were forced to walk upon me, up and down in ceaseless toil, rolling barrels, tending horses alongside the paler lives but as inhuman to those English as their own dark shadows.

Once, in these days when the English cut trees and built fences, cut rock and built walls, and mica sparked like electricity along my spine, one of the unfree dark ones ran away. She came from a northern estate called

Epsom Farm. Unlike so many, she was running *south*, running into the heart of Eastern Shore slavery, to find her twin sister, unfree, and rumored to be toiling on the coast, if she was still alive. The escaped girl ran at night, panic quick in her bare feet.

Another girl was also running, a tall girl, one of the last tall ones. She came from far, a town called Conestoga, where pale people massacred the Susquehannocks, beating them bluntly to death. She was young and fast, had managed to weave nimbly under attack, and, despite losing blood from her head and shoulder, she was running still, exhausted. They reached me, these two girls, on the same dark pre-dawn morning and by fortune both were thirsty and clever enough to presume that my valley sheltered a river, running water.

They were afraid of each other at first and hid in the shadows, watching each other as the early sun tinted the tree trunks pink and yellow. Until the sun was colorless and bright above they watched each other, both still and terrified. Then the tall one, still bloody from her escape far north, fell down, down onto my earth, down as if dead, her weak-sour breathing only lightly warming my soil. The dark girl startled, staggered out of the tangled bush, looked, went to the other, touched her, smelt her breath warm but rank with hunger, dragged the tall body to my stream's edge and cupped water to her face, washing dry blood into water, cupping water with her hand to the other girl's mouth.

The two stayed by my stream for several days, awkward with each other, but good partners in survival. They hid together under branches leant against a wide fallen oak. They ate purslane to clear their sticky mouths—citrus astringent, green tasting, and sweet. They caught squirrels and small fish. They found the fallen acorns, used fire, rock, to crack open to the meat inside.

In an early evening, windy, the trees rushing their leaves, they were here. Two girls, one dark, one tall, around a small fire in the woods near my stream, working to shelter the fire from the wind. A pale man on a horse came upon them. He'd come down from my spine along a deer track to the river. He too was looking for water. The girls hadn't heard him because the trees were rushing so loud, because the river was singing, because the fire made its constant crickling. They did not hear the horse with man until they also saw him.

He saw them, stopping his red horse so sharp she huffed, tossed her head in protest, thumped a hind hoof down in complaint. He saw them. All still, all still, even it seemed like the wind and its dancing leaves held themselves in waiting. Two girls, a man on a horse.

The man appraises what he is seeing and surmises that the puzzle of these girls, one a run-away slave, one an Indian, add up to danger for him. So he takes his double-barreled pistol from his side, cocks it while his mare begins to wheel, knowing from the click she's just heard the terrible sounds to come, and shoots. Once, cocks again, a second shot. Then he re-holsters his gun and rides through the scrubby growth upriver to drink where there is no fresh blood in the water.

Those two girls.

Blood running to water and soil, white bones in the sun: white and hollow like all the bones.

There's a party in the cemented-over yard of a row house on Willow Street a long stretch of seasons and summers later. Large people, laughter, chairs with aluminum legs and plastic webbing for the backs and seat. Music inside the house turned loud to thrum the air outside into vivid noise. A grill with hot charcoal, the smell of lighter fluid. Plastic soda bottles orange and green. Beer cans. Sweet liquors. Bright afternoon sun. Blue blue sky. The laughing people do not hear the silver car over the music. It turns from York Road, down the hill and chokes itself to a stop outside the loud thrumming house, the searing concrete, the crowd of large people. The silver car idles.

The car's driver looks, and pulls his black gun from its waiting place on the seat beside him, leans it out the car window. Bullets spray into the yard, over the grill, through the orange and green soda bottles, through the large people and their laughter. The gun stops, the car screams as it accelerates away. The loud music inside the house still thrums the air outside while blood runs fast in all directions; it cannot come home because of the concrete.

Blood streams, vivid in the bright heat. It pools, dark and shiny. The air smells of car exhaust, lighter fluid and blood. Sirens, sirens coming.

Tomorrow at two in the afternoon, Em will knock on my door and we will walk over to Ma's house. Why did she ask? Why did I agree? It now seems crazy to me that I was so very angry in the garden, in the thorny rosebushes. She's still got the marks on her forehead, and there she was asking me all innocent, her dogs wagging their tails at me. I guess I said yes because I didn't want to be unreasonable about the loaded-with-significance umlaut that she knows nothing about. I don't know. None of it makes sense to me, and reaching to understand why it all feels so darned *inevitable* just makes me tired, like my limbs each weigh twenty pounds more than usual all of a sudden.

I sigh, put the paper MOM's bag on the kitchen counter, and think, trying to be clear with myself: On the one hand, I don't know why Em is interested in the house. On the other, now that the thing's in front of me, planned, it doesn't feel too bad, or even too unexpected. It's been a while since I checked on the inside of the house. It's a good idea for me to go look anyway. It's just something to be organized and got through. No big deal, right?

I am still wet: I got caught in the thunder and rain on the way to the store. I waited the worst of it out inside the store, too cold in the chilled grocery, and my shoulders, knees and ankles are still wet now, the fabric of my clothing dark with rain. Where are the keys to Ma's house, even? I have to find them. Also, the crowbar to take boards off the door. There's no light in there. I should bring a flashlight too, and a hammer and nails, to put the boards back up when we're done. That's going to be a lot of work: boards off and then boards back on again. Maybe Tyrell can come, help, provide moral support. It'd be better if he were going to be there.

My mental list is ready, but actually assembling all the gear will have to wait for a few hours.

First, dry clothes, and then I better call on Peter and David, the Ivorian auto dealer guys. They're expecting me this afternoon. I was up late again last night with their books. Something's not checking out quite right, which is juicy. They've got income they are trying to hide. It's a numbers game for me: I have some solutions, some ways to hide things innocently enough in an array of different tallies.

An hour later, in my still wet sneakers but with clean and dry, albeit battered, black jeans and a dry red Old Navy sweatshirt, I am at the door of "Auto Export To Africa" on the ground floor of the big white marble building on York road. The hallway carpet is yellow flecked with orange and brown, the hall floor itself uneven. It smells of stale milk in here. I have my umbrella in one hand (I am not getting rained on again today, dang it), my laptop in its case slung over my shoulder and my free hand raised to knock on the shut door, when Peter swings the door open, outward, swiftly and I have to move quickly out of the way not to get banged by it.

"*Dan*-ny!" he greets me. "I saw you already by the window! Please, come," gesturing for me to enter, big smile on his face.

Their office has a low ceiling, and a big window with bars over it facing York. The window reveals that this room is actually at a slightly lower level than the parking lot out front. There's more of the same yellow and brown flecked carpet. There are two desks, one facing the window and one floating right in the middle of the room. Both desks have big beige, outdated desk top computers on them (massive tube monitors, clunky towers and heavy keyboards) and both have enormous black office chairs. There are no shelves or paintings on the walls. No plants. There is a low, scuffed black leather armchair in the corner, and this is what Peter directs me towards.

"Please, sit. Come!"

When I sit, the seat of the low lounge chair sags downwards, so I am even lower, even more confined, my knees up higher than my waist so that I feel like a grasshopper that's tipped over backwards to balance on its pointy behind. Peter sits at the desk in the middle of the room, puts his hands behind his head and starts pivoting his big black chair from side to side.

"*Dan*-ny. How are all things? You want some coffee? A coke? Some chips?"

"No. Thanks. I'm good. David joining us today?"

"Ah, no. David is not in today. Saturday, you know. Technically we do not open on the weekend."

"Right, OK. I was hoping to talk to you both, you see." It's a delicate thing this conversation I need to have with them. I need to communicate to them that I know, and that I don't mind, I don't care, but that they aren't doing a good job of covering their tracks.

"It's OK, *Dan*-ny! I can pass along all that we talk about today, alright? Have a coke. I am going to take one." Peter takes a room temperature can out if his desk drawer and offers it to me. He fishes out another one for himself.

We drink tepid coke, which seems extra fizzy at this temperature, while I awkwardly open and start my laptop on my lap. I put the fizzy soda on the floor next to my low chair. The laptop whirrs. Eventually I have 4 windows open, each with a different spreadsheet.

"See, now, Peter, I think you are doing great business in the Côte d'Ivoire! You know. *Great*. Lots of profits! But" I lean forward and with difficulty lurch upwards out of the black chair to show him the screen; I show him the numbers on the first sheet, the columns that don't add up highlighted in blue. Peter furrows his brow and squints. Before he can respond I toggle windows:

"Now you could move shipping costs here, and put

the taxes on a different sheet, like this." I toggle more to show him. "And then," showing the third sheet "you can have it all add up. It's mostly legal like this, or easy enough to say you made an honest error if you need to." And then I stop talking about it. I pass him the laptop and pick up my soda. "Nice coke. Thank you."

"Oh, you are welcome, *Dan*-ny my friend," Peter says absentmindedly, toggling from one spreadsheet to the next, head ducked down to focus on the screen in his hands. "Can you give me these on a flash driver?" He puts my laptop on his desk and starts rooting around in his desk drawer, the one the coke cans came from, presumably looking for a flash drive to pass me.

"Already done, Mr. P!" I fish a flash drive out of my pocket and pass it to him. My name's not on any of these things, and there's no IP address involved because the documents aren't coming from an email. Even if they were, it would be really hard to trace back to my laptop. I'm sure anything is possible, but it's pretty unlikely any of this will come back to haunt me.

Peter hands my laptop back. "Can you excuse me for a minute, *Dan*-ny? I must give David a call after all and tell him about your work, OK?"

I stand in the uneven hall while Peter talks to David on his cell in a mix of French and maybe Ashante? I don't know the West African languages at all. His tone is worried, and then Peter says "ah, ah, ah" repeatedly, like he is checking off items on a list David is reading to him over the phone. After several minutes of talking, and then several worrying minutes of silence during which I wonder if I am being cheated somehow in there, Peter swings the door sharply open again.

"Come, come. Please!" he says, "We are so Happy! You have done a nice job, ah? Thank-you *Dan*-ny. It is good to have such good friends." He reaches to shake my hand, and I see cradled in his palm a tight roll of bills. I shake hands, the roll is transferred to my palm and I put it in my pocket. Nice. Unexpected, but very nice. I'll count it later.

"Now," says Peter briskly "have you seen my new car? It is a BMW. Very beautiful! New one. Can I drive you anywhere this afternoon?"

"Hey, man! Show me your car. I'd love to see it. I don't need a ride. I just live down the street."

So I get to see Peter's black, low, immaculate BMW, and then I saunter off down York road, happy to have this delicate diplomatic work out of the way, happy to have money in my pocket, and happiest of all to have put Em, the house, and with the house Ma and Linnie, far out of my mind for a stretch of time. The respite is only brief though. I am still burping warm coke bubbles as thoughts about tomorrow also start bubbling inside me.

As I walk down York, the sky still brightening overhead as the rain clouds blow off, the pavement still wet and puddled, I feel more and more keyed-up about tomorrow. As it gets sunnier outside, I feel cloudier in.

I don't want to handle being in there, Ma's house, with Em, by myself. Ma's house! Dang. Something about the idea checking it out makes me excited. That's surprising. I haven't wanted to go into Ma's house in years. Now I want to, hopefully with Tyrell. Why? I can't imagine there will have been any *good* developments in there since I last looked. Things can only be getting more, not less, decrepit. What do I imagine I am going to see?

The words "sure thing" had slid out of my mouth, easy as honey off a hot spoon. If I am honest with myself, it feels like some kind of Event is coming, something dramatic, a strange once in a lifetime type moment.

It's getting warm outside now that the sun is out, too warm for my spooked mood.

Rather than heading straight home, I walk over to Tyrell's place. His house fronts onto York, just south of Coldspring. There used to be a hair braiding place, "Nappy by Nature," on the ground floor but that went out of business a few years ago, so it's a boarded up glass shop front now, with the narrow door (locked) that leads to the stairs up to his place recessed back between the brick walls. Going in there is like going into a tiny alley, and it always reeks of pee because the private, hidden space is so inviting for folk who need a quick release.

I knock. No answer. I knock twice more and then wait. After a couple of minutes I knock again, and finally I can hear footfalls on the wooden stairs inside and Tyrell:

"Yeah, yeah. I'm a-comin'. Just give me a minute. On my way."

"Hey, man! Sorry to bring you all the way down."

Tyrell greets me with a hug and thump on the back and I follow him upstairs: a narrow flight, another door, also locked, another flight of narrow stairs, and finally a living room with a big plasma TV along one wall and couches taking up the length of each of the other three. Tyrell's daughter's kids, his grandkids, are there. The eldest, a young man named J'Andre, is almost eighteen now, and he is sprawled with his knees wide, big red Nikes on his feet. The TV is blaring: a cartoon with anime characters with huge eyes. J'Andre has got the younger kids with him, two girls. I can never remember their ages or names, but they are under the ten year mark, the two of them. They are playing with a stiff white toy kitten they've balanced on a remote control toy skateboard. It mews artificially and the board rattles across the uneven wood floor.

"Hi everyone, Mr. J'Andre," I say. No one responds. I follow Tyrell through into the tiny, grimy kitchen.

It smells close in there. Something has been cooking for a long time. I lift a pot lid and see collards, cooked to a grey-green mush. The smell makes my stomach rise. I replace the lid, and decide I'll be quick with Tyrell. Turns out, I'd like to get out of here as soon as I can.

"Oh, uh huh," says Tyrell, nodding to the mush "We're making family dinner for tonight, Sat'day night family times!"

"I won't keep you." I briefly explain about Em, and the house, and ask if Tyrell can come along tomorrow. At first he says no. He can't. He's doing the church thing again. But I guess he can tell from the look of me that it's important. Plus he's curious too. Ma's house has been a secret for so long. So then he says he'll leave church at lunch, come home and change, and meet me at my house at one thirty for a quick glass of tea before Em stops by to get us. He looks concerned, pats me on the shoulder, keeps saying "OK then, OK then, OK then," like he's reassuring me.

When I leave, trip-hop-bopping down all the narrow stairs on my own this time, I am relieved and not just to get away from the warm collard stench. It's good that Tyrell will be there tomorrow. I am glad about it. I can almost imagine the afternoon being a bit fun.

Eᴍ

I have the spinning dream on Saturday night and I wake from it into the mid-nighttime darkness of my bedroom. I still sleep in the room that was mine as a child, not the "master" which I use as a guest bedroom, or, more honestly, a place to dump things I don't know what to do with. My window lets in the streetlight from Kerneway Ave, even with the thick blue cotton curtain shut. So, I wake with the diffuse grey of streetlight coming through. But maybe I am not awake? I hear a baby coughing: it sounds wet, mucusy. It makes me panicky. I feel urgently that the baby must be sat up or it will choke.

My brain strains to come awake and be rational. Maybe it's one of the dogs? No, the dogs are both asleep on my bed. I keep hearing the coughs, and I struggle to get out from the sheets that tangle my legs, struggle to get out from the weight of the dogs on the sheets. Then I am standing, and staggering into the hall, still in the dark, towards the wet, desperate sound of that young child.

I flip the hall light switch on, the light piercing so I have to hold my hand over my eyes. The coughing stops. There's silence and then the sound of Blue tumbling heavily from the bed and yawning—a long "ack" with a squeak at the end, a distinctive dog-yawn—as he stretches on his way to see what I am doing. I lean against the wall for a long time, trying to figure out if I am awake or asleep, or maybe this is sleepwalking, which is something entirely new to me.

I am uneasy, confused: what the fuck was *that*? I go into each of the upstairs rooms, turning on lights, looking for an explanation. Both dogs follow me, wearily. I check the main floor too, the basement. I leave all the lights on. Finally I go to the bathroom to pee, and go back to bed where I lay, awake, until my alarm goes off at five forty-five.

Sunday.

A quick walk in the dark for the dogs, just the Kerneway/ Coldspring loop. It is surprisingly cold given yesterday's muggy storm in the morning and warm afternoon. I have gone out without a coat. I'm glad to hustle home in the dark. My orange juice chills me even more, and I shiver while chewing a handful of almonds. Then I head off to Towson to teach. I feel as though I am watching myself from two feet up and slightly to the left: I am almost, but not quite, in myself.

Fortunately the morning vinyasa class is small— only five people today, none of them friends or students I know very well personally, and none of them chatty in the greyness of the early morning. I leave the studio silent as we set up, no music today, no incense. I leave the lights off. No "ohm" to lead in, just me calling the inhale and exhale. The atmosphere is sepulchral, reverential.

Though vinyasa can, and generally should, vary its sequencing, I rely entirely on the ashtanga primary series today, pushing the students to keep them in each pose for no longer than five breaths. I call inhale and exhale through sun salutations A and B, forward folds, trikonasana, the whole sequence as far as navasana, boat pose. By that point, the students are sweating, shaking, not following my breathing cues. They collapse gratefully into an abbreviated closing sequence of shoulder stand and supine twists.

"Whoa, that was a tough one" a wiry young student says after class. "Tough. But good."

"Mmm." I say, and smile slightly. I don't feel the release I usually feel when I teach. I still feel weird, displaced. I am glad the room is still quiet and dim.

"I like it. *Super* intense way to start a Sunday!"

"Namaste." I say, though I hate myself as I do it. I am not an Indian swami, so why the pseudo-spiritual teacher-ego-guru mumbo-jumbo? I don't have the wherewithal today to fall into my well-worn mental debate with myself about the rightness or wrongness of yoga (an ancient Sanskrit and Hindu tradition) in modern American fitness culture.

I wonder if Bev is at Atwater's. She often is on a Sunday morning. She meets her politico friend Mary there and they talk insider gossip about the Maryland House of Delegates and the congressional districts. Generally, in my experience, this gossip devolves into rants about redlining. It's stuff I should care about, but can't make myself pay attention to.

It'd be nice to see Bev. It'd be nice to talk to someone.

Some caffeine wouldn't be a bad thing. I guess I want to tell someone about my afternoon plans too. Not that I distrust Danny, but someone should know that I am heading into a boarded up house in a dubious neighborhood, just in case I don't come back. I could text Bev and ask if she's coffee-ing today, but I don't want to: maybe she's not there, or maybe she doesn't want me to intrude, or maybe I don't want to formally meet her, but would rather just stop in on her for a few minutes and then bail, leave, without having to wait out her conversations with Mary. I'll just swing by and look.

From the traffic circle in Towson I drive straight south on York Road, all the way to Belvedere Square, a nice development a block south of Northern Parkway, across from the refurbished Senator movie theater and the new Canadian burger place that does a gut-busting Quebecois *poutine.* The wine bar in Belvedere is a bit frou frou for me—men in ironed collared shirts and blue jeans, women in floral blazers and kitten heels—but Atwater's is a great bakery. Sadly, all of their soups taste roughly the same, though sometimes there's a stand-out crab bisque or gumbo. Still, it's a nice place to get a scone, and sit amidst the cheerful bustle. It has good windows.

Traffic in their parking lot is a disaster so I park at

a meter on the street. I can see Bev is sitting at a table outside despite the damp chill in the air this morning. There are two big tan ceramic coffee cups on the table, and Mary is just coming out the door to join her with two vast smoothies in clear plastic cups, one pale pink, the other pale green. She passes Bev the pink one, and Bev is sucking hard, cheeks caving in on themselves as she tries to get the thick slush up the straw, when I walk up.

"Pink! Nice color Bev!" I tease, "Hi."

"Oh my god, Em! Long time no see." Bev stands awkwardly around the edge of the table and gives me a one-armed hug. "What are you doing here?"

"Thought I'd stop to grab a tea and a breakfast sandwich. I just finished a class. Hiya Mary. How's it going?" I nod towards Mary, who is looking great in her green cords, orange sweater, and carefully coiffed afro. I wonder if she's had her teeth done. They look so even. I don't think they looked that way before.

"Join us?" Mary asks.

"Uh, yeah. Just for a bit." I hate myself for being so fake casual. "I'll just go in and order something."

Atwater's is swarming with people and overwhelming with cacophony. Inside there's table service at two tops, four tops and the beautiful glossy oak bar that runs along the side of the pastry outlet. There's also a counter where you can walk up to order. Near the back and around the periphery of the market's indoor space other vendors also sell things to eat: locally made chocolates, sauerkraut and fermented beverages, udon, cheese pies, fresh-pressed fruit and vegetable juices, and even Louisiana style pizza. This morning every seat is taken, every establishment has a line.

At the Atwater's counter I get in line behind a slim and beautiful auburn-maned woman with her son. He's maybe four or so, with blond curls and a runny nose. He keeps grabbing the saran-wrapped biscotti and cookies off the counter and stuffing them in his mouth. She removes them and puts them back on the counter for some unsuspecting patron to buy even though they are wet with her son's saliva. I cringe, revulsed. She looks defeated, exhausted. I notice that her cherry red raw silk shawl has something whitish caked on in it a long pale smear. She pleads with him: "Jackie, no. Please. Please stop. Please." And my cringe becomes a judgmental sneer of distaste for them both.

Because I have been watching them, it takes me a while to see that Tania is seated at the long wooden bar just to my left, with her sketchbook, working on something, some design for the young hipster man (plaid shirt, moustache) sitting next to her. As I see her, she looks up, pausing mid conversation with the hipster. In looking up, she sees me. I gawp, she cocks her head quizzically, lightly mocking me, and then blows me a kiss.

God fucking damn it. Smalltimore. Big enough that

you never run into the people you want to see (though I did just engineer a meeting with Bev) and small enough that you ALWAYS run into just the person you'd rather not. By the time I have my tea ("Brahmin" : is there not something politically incorrect about naming Darjeeling tea after the pre-eminent Hindu caste?) and the scone I have selected in lieu of waiting for a sandwich, I am sweaty and irritable with trying to act as thought Tania's presence hasn't rattled me. My nervous sweat smells bad, and the heat of it, of me, makes the poison ivy on my legs itch. I work hard to control myself: I don't want to be standing here sweaty and scratching like some kind of deranged person. Today I really *feel* like a deranged person, but that's not something I want Tania to see. Tania keeps working, sketching this whole time, with a small contented smile on her brightly painted lips. I am tremendously relieved when I can go back outside.

Bev is mid-rant, gesticulating with her hands:

"I can't *believe* it. She's just such a douche if she thinks another 'pop-up maker-space' for white artsy types is what Baltimore needs."

Mary is laughing hard, rocking back and forth with it,

"I know, I know. Right? Ha! Hi Em, we thought you'd never make it out alive! It got fierce in there, huh?"

It's a relief to sit with these women. Bev is cranky, always, and I love her for it. Mary's laugh is a nice offset: they are a good pair. We chat, I eat my scone and wish it had more dry apricots in it, I like those, and that it was a bit bigger too: I am still hungry when I finish it. I see Tania leave with her plaid-clad client and so I sit longer than I intended. Eventually, as I am leaving, standing up to go, I say,

"Hey Bev, can you give me a call tonight, maybe around six? I am looking at an abandoned house this afternoon and it's sketchy."

"Yeah, OK. What?? Why are you looking? You going to buy? I thought you liked your Kerneway place."

"Nah, not buying, just looking. Curious and nosy."

"Uh, OK. Sure." Bev looks concerned. "Dude, you look tired too." she says, "What's up?"

"Oh, the old house and the tiredness aren't related," I say, "At least I think they aren't!" It's meant to be a joke, but something clutches in my intestines as I say it. "No no," I insist, "the house is just curiosity. The tiredness is because I've been having nightmares."

"Dude!" Bev says again, and dramatically pulls the chair that I had been sitting on back out from the table so that I will sit down again. I do, but I sit perched on the edge of the seat, hands wedged nervously between my knees, suddenly unable to make eye contact. Again, I can smell my own nervous sweat-stink, the result of seeing Tania inside now refreshed by this conversation. I know, of course, that Bev loves dreams. In college she geeked out on the bizarreness of Freudian dream interpretation. She loves to play-analyze dreams.

"Spill," she demands. And so I do. I tell her and Mary all about the spinning dream, and the version in which I am a small boy, and the squirrel dream, and add, hesitantly, last night's odd hallucination of a baby coughing.

Bev is uncharacteristically quiet when I stop talking. Mary is just looking at me, wide-eyed.

"How long has this been going on for?"

"Oh, since mid-summer. Julyish." It's October now.

"Jesus, Em. That's a lot of nightmares. Did something happen in July?"

"No, uh. Not really. Nothing traumatic anyway." That's roughly when Girlfriend ran away, I think to myself.

"Well, that sounds like serious messed up shit, my dear." Bev says, affectionately. "Too much for me. Let's find you a good therapist, shall we? Oh! Actually I know a one if you are willing to go to Owings Mills. She's a dog person. Adopted a big mastiff-mix foster from me. She seems *great*."

I nod, dumbly, in the face of Bev's emphasis and enthusiasm. I have no intention of going to a therapist. Before I leave, Bev insists she call earlier this afternoon, four thirty, not six, and she makes me give her the address of the house on Alhambra.

Cars make it harder for me to connect things. My energy cannot make contact.

In their cars, the downward life of them does not flow to me.

Tarmac. Concrete. Shoes. All diminish the force that flows. I yearn for them to walk on my soil with their bare soles. In their cars I almost lose them. They speed over. They don't feel me, and I ache. I feel them as shadows.

The dogwalker drives south this important day, south along the York Road from Northern Parkway to Coldspring. I know she will park her car in the shade, and later she will walk.

It is only in the most recent two or three of human lifetimes that the trees have entirely gone. The York Road was widened, so men cut trees down along it. The row houses: men cut trees. Though the street named Willow never had willows, it did at one time have seventeen redbud trees whose purple spring blooms burst straight from their smooth dark branches. The row houses consumed them completely. The chestnuts became sick with a blackening fungus. They grew wet sores on their bark, and the sap leaked from them. They died quickly, mere seasons from each other. Some of them ancient, and all dead within a few cycles of warm to cold to warm.

A few seasons later, the small firehouse was closed,

the one that had horses first, and then trucks in the wedge of land alongside Bellona and the York Road. After the firehouse became dusty and dry, without water, many of my tall, wide pin oaks were caught in fire. They would not have burned if water could have come to them more quickly. They would not have burned if the buildings did not catch so easily like straw. But the firehouse was empty, and a big fire roared all along the low narrow shop buildings—shops and places to buy food—all along York near Woodbourne. How quickly the trees were lost.

There is a surviving ancient oak, and an ancient pine, by the Govans Presbyterian cemetery where some of their bodies lie in my earth. There was once a white oak here too, adjacent to the weathered stone grave markers. It was planted the year James Govane was interred. By the time James Govane *Howard* was laid in my soil, it was already a tall, shade-giving beauty.   Tiny infant William Govane Law was laid here too, with the fallen leaves of the white oak giving him a rustling shroud of orange and yellow.

The tree grew taller and more lovely, sheltering a preschool that flourished in its shade, hearing the voices of young happy play and screaming, the cries with skinned knees, feeling the occasional, accidental seep of a child's blood into the soil after a raucous injury borne out of living hard and well.

In one early summer, in the era of the dogwalker

and thin man, I had a storm rush through me fast and surprising. A storm of great speed, with forceful winds and rain that spat heavy warm drops. My derecho was short, unexpected by them. It was a rare explosion of weather, blowing out the electric lights and making them all feel the heat of summer coming on. Govane's tree fell in the storm, as did so many.

Yet all must be let go in order that new things can grow. I know this: the shadowy shade must fall down in order to bring light to my soil. New things will grow. I wait to see what new things.

There are some new plantings within the last springs, saplings caught in tiny squares left for them. They are growing slowly. Too slowly. They do not have enough room for their roots under the tarmac. They do not have enough water because it cannot flow to them when it rains. Concrete and asphalt keep the water from them. Cars make chemicals that trouble their leaves. Sometimes cars run up right into them. Sirens come.

Too few trees, and too much garbage. People lean from their cars, lean down, not to touch me but to put their dirty plastics, perpetually slick and shiny no matter how many seasons rub them, down upon me. I am leafed with garbage.

Along the York Road, so small the speeding cars can't see it, so small the limping only notice if they pause to rest, is an abandoned city block, small, but thick with trees. Some humans painted a sign in wobbly letters, pink and green, "Urban Forest," aspiring for clean air, for a place in which the woodpeckers can land, for a spot the moths can shelter from the leaden dust wind. Some humans pee through the fence and laugh at such a small forest. I cannot blame them for laughing over this: it *is* such a small forest.

They make this joke. They make it out of feeling separate: a fenced forest, closed off, as if they need to be protected from it.

But we are of each other. Their place is me.

I can hear Blue and Girlfriend barking inside the house before I have even finished parking. They are making an almighty racket. I see why when I look to the big holly bush flanking the front door.

"Will!" My hearts jumps with pleasure and concern. I assess as I get out of my car and go up to hug him: he looks like shit. Where are his glasses? One of his eyes is swollen shut, and he's got snot congealed where unkempt nose hair meets uncontrolled hair growth on his upper lip. I hug him, carefully keeping my head averted so he doesn't kiss my face. I love him, but the mucus is a bit much. He smells bad, like dirty clothes and cigarettes. His lips have chalky-sticky spit gluing them together at the corners.

"Jesus, Dude! How are you? I am sorry I missed you that other morning. I need to be better about answering my phone. Actually, I *have* been better since missing you that time. Anyway, come on in to the house for a bit."

I am hopeful. This time, surely, he will come in. Surely. I so badly want to heal over the rift I feel between us. As I am ushering him forwards towards the door I calculate how much time before I go to see Danny (about an hour). Will backs towards the holly. He's not coming in. I feel disappointed, crushed, snubbed. He's here, but it's not about seeing me. It's never about seeing me. I get annoyed, defensive.

"Nah, Pups. I'm not coming in. Just wanted to stop and say hello."

I open the front door to let the dogs come out with us and to avoid making eye contact so that Will doesn't see the tears that are smarting in my eyes. I sit on the front step. Will joins me. Patting the happy, wagging, panting dogs and still not looking directly at him, I ask:

"What happened to your glasses? Your face?"

His answer is evasive.

"Oh, you know. Rough living."

"No shit." I wonder who caught him, and for what.

I know already, knew already from the moment I heard the dogs barking, what he's really here for and it only takes a couple more phatic and empty conversational moves before we're there.

"Hey, Pup, I don't suppose . . ."

"Yeah, of course. Let me see what I've got."

I've got a twenty, a five, and four ones in my wallet. I've got twenty-two quarters in my glove compartment. I give him all of it. I wonder if it was worth the trip to him, I wonder if it does him any good. If more, or less, would be better. Then he's gone, and I already miss him. I miss the old Will. I miss my brother, the one who was like a parent to me, who read to me and played with me. I want a hug from *that* long-ago Will. I want to tell *that* Will about my dreams. I want to cry to him and ask for his help. I want him to be there for me, but he isn't.

I still have plenty of time for a shower, and to make myself an egg sandwich to fill the space the scone never filled. I cry in the shower, the sense of loss familiar in my chest. I am tired, exhausted, from lack of sleep and a day that has already been too emotional, but I am also full of conflicting nervous energy. I am increasingly keyed up, jittery, in anticipation of the afternoon to come.

Danny

One in the afternoon and I am sitting in the kitchen, waiting for Tyrell. I am jiggling from the balls of my feet. My knees toggle rapidly up and down with it. I am tight and nervous. I just want to get on with the afternoon. In my backpack I've got the best nails I could find in the house and a hammer to put the plywood back on whatever we've decided to open, three flashlights so we can look around when we're in there and a baggie of *springerle* in case anyone gets hungry. Key's in my pocket, crow bar is waiting just inside the front door. I stand up abruptly and stride into the dim, windowless sitting room that's at the center of my row house to look at the little digital clock that's part of the DVD player's display: three minutes past one. Jeez Louise, would it kill Tyrell to be early? My cellphone rings and I startle before rooting it out of my pocket, clumsy from trying to do so too quickly. It's not Tyrell's number, but Peter's at Auto Export.

"Hello, Daniel speaking," Those German air-base years really influenced how I answer a phone. I like the formality of 'Hello', and I like the clarity of announcing myself. No one else I ever call answers a phone like this anymore. It's more typical to get a 'Yeah?' but I am always a little taken aback by the rudeness of a barked monosyllable.

"Dan-*ny*! It's Peter here, from Auto Export to Africa."

"Oh, hi, Peter. What's up?"

"Dan-*ny*, David and I, we would like to put your name and social security number on the excellent tax work you did for us, OK? Can you give the right spelling to me and the number also?" His voice is innocent and cheerful, like he doesn't know he's putting the illegal figuring of their numbers on me.

I'd like to say *No Way! No, I cannot!* but what I do say is "Oh, now. That's OK. You paid me! I've got credit enough for my time, thank-you. And thank-you so much for your business! Much appreciated, as always. Let me know when there's something else I can do for you, OK?" I bet they wish they hadn't paid up all at once. Maybe this need to make someone explicitly, legally, responsible for the filed returns didn't occur to them until today.

"Oh, but David says it is very important. We *must* he says. It is the best thing." I'll bet David does: covering his own exposed rear by putting mine on the line, nuh-uh. Good for David for pushing this, though. I wonder if he's the brains behind their business and Peter is just the front man, the smiling face. Maybe David should have worked a Saturday, I think wryly. I am relieved he didn't though: I got paid *and* they don't have my particulars.

"Hey, OK. That's great. I can't just now though, alright? You've caught me right in the middle of something. I'll call you back a little later this afternoon, OK?" And I press the red phone icon to end the call. Dang. I have no intention of calling them back. I liked having them as clients, but there'll be no more work with them now. I am sure as shooting not giving them my full name and my social to put on those cooked numbers. At least I got paid before this happened, I remind myself, again. I am also glad I never let Peter drive me home: it's good he doesn't actually know where I live. My heart is beating too quick. I wrack and wrack my brains to think of any identifying markers on that flash drive I gave them: I can't think of anything that would effectively incriminate me.

I have a bad feeling that Peter, or more likely David, won't let this drop.

Tyrell shows up at twenty after one. He's a good friend, sensitive to the unusualness of this afternoon's plan; I am relieved he's early. I give him a one-armed hug and we go into the kitchen for a glass of tea.

"How was church?"

"Oh, you know. Lots of singing, lots of big hats, lots of babies crying and a donation plate under my nose every five minutes."

I laugh. It's a relief to let some of my nervous tension out that way.

"Nyasha must like to have you there though, right?"

"Yeah. She's come over all family values these days. She likes it. It's good, I guess. We're all there together. Bonding and close. It's good. Sometimes my bony butt gets sore on those hard plastic chairs though, I tell you.

It's a long day, a whole Sunday at Church. Nice to have an excuse to get out for a few hours and walk around!" Tyrell smirks. I laugh again and slap him on the shoulder.

"Glad you're here, man. Real glad." My phone chirps, and I see it is Peter again. I silence it and put it back in my pocket. I don't realize until after I've done so that I am standing on the balls of my feet, nervous. Tyrell raises his eyebrows at me.

"Hot date?"

"Yuh-huh." I slap his shoulder again, harder this time.

Eᴍ

By the time I have showered, gotten dressed and made myself something to eat it is a quarter to two. My eyes feel raw from tiredness and crying over Will. The sandwich on its little grey plate looks delicious: rye toast, a fried egg with cheese melted on top, some jalepeno slices and slices of one last flavorful tomato from the stubborn and persistent plant in the pot on the back porch, the one that is still fruiting despite the colder weather. It looks appetizing, but my tongue is dry in my mouth. Fifteen minutes until I am supposed to meet Danny. I have to leave soon. Standing at the kitchen counter, I take a bite and force it down, chewing mechanically. I take another and then put the sandwich back on its plate: I can't eat right now, even though I should. I force down two more big bites, ignoring them as much as possible, chewing just enough to swallow the food down.

Then I futz around getting ready. Coat or no coat? Blundstones or sneakers? Bring a bag with a flashlight in it, or just what I can put in my pockets? It's like I am leaving for several days, not for an hour or so on a walk down the block. I settle on blundstones, and a fleece zip up with a slim but powerful LED flashlight jammed in the pocket and a hat, one of those knitted things my Canadian yoga student Charlie calls a "toque." By the time I leave, I am running a couple of minutes late. That's OK. Better not to be too punctual.

I am practically jumping around the living room by ten of two, so Tyrell suggests we go wait on the porch. I grab my back pack, and the crowbar, and we head out. I am having trouble sitting still. I keep looking at my phone to see the time, but every time I look at it I am reminded of the message from Peter, which is just the last thing I want to deal with. It's after two when Em finally strides down the street. Tyrell and I meet her on the sidewalk.

"Hey, Em. You remember Tyrell?"

Tyrell waves a theatrical little wave, right hand flapping blurry from side to side, like Bugs Bunny waving to Elmer Fudd. Em remains unsmiling.

"Yeah. Hi Tyrell, didn't know you were coming. Afternoon Danny."

"Ready?"

"Yeah."

The sidewalk is narrow, and even on a Sunday there are cars coming by way too fast. Clearly the three of us can't walk side-by-side, so there's some awkwardness in figuring out what order we're going to walk in. I, politely, offer Em to go first, but she declines, so I take the lead and we march off down Coldspring. I decided ahead of time that we would cross York at the light and walk down the hill, turning left on Alhambra even though time and development have broken it up; it cuts weirdly north-east so that to actually stay on it as far as Ma's house we'll have to turn right onto Radnor for a block and then left again to come back onto Alhambra. In spite of its detours, I think it is the shortest route, but it keeps us right by the busy-ness of Coldspring for the first part of our walk, on a narrow sidewalk. As a result, we have to walk single-file, and there's no conversation. It's awkward.

Tyrell walks right behind me, Em at the back. When I look over behind me, Tyrell's shoulders are up and stiff, and Em looks like she's faking being casual, looking at the houses and cars passing like a kid pretending she hasn't just stolen the last cookie. On one side of us there are disintegrating faux tudor row houses, on the other the traffic roars past, churning up dust and trash, everything from cigarillo wrappers to abandoned Big Gulp cups with broken glass in between. At least the early afternoon sun is just behind us. Turning onto the first, mercifully quiet, stretch of Alhambra, we stay single file, still stunned perhaps by the unpleasantness of walking along Coldspring. Then on Radnor there are brick row houses with their windows and doors boarded shut with cheap OSB. Someone has tacked a cardboard sign against one of these closed doors: "Stop Killing Each Other." It's a reminder that we are in gang-land over here. There are shootings. It would be easy to be in the wrong place at the wrong time. Once we turn onto the last stretch of Alhambra, things open out. There are houses here, run down but big, on large plots of land. There are trees, overgrown bushes, impressive writhing vines, shade. There's no traffic so I start walking on the road. Em speeds up to flank my left, Tyrell my right. The woman smoker in the house across the street from Ma's is on her porch today, this time wearing a puffy purple Ravens coat. I see her see us coming, raise her eyebrows apparently so as to convey both surprise and distaste, and heave herself up from her plastic chair, flick her cigarette butt off the porch into the overgrown bushes, and head back inside.

Finally we are at Ma's house. The garden looks OK after my cutting it back: wild still, but not so much like it's swallowing everything. The cooler weather is slowing the plants down now too. The sky's grey overhead and in the places where the peeling paint has exposed the wood, the siding is dark with moisture, almost black. The plywood over the downstairs doors and windows seems swollen and wet too. It looks heavy.

"OK, y'all." I am nervous, hamming it up. I never say "y'all" and we are not a collective but rather a pair of friends (me and Tyrell) and a pair of people acting weird around each other (me and Em) with a guardian of sorts (Tyrell). "Where shall we start? Front door, back door, French doors?"

"Back," says Tyrell loudly, with a bit of a bounce as he says it. "That one's not got boards, right?"

"They've all got boards" I say.

"Front" says Em, decisively, "Stairs up to the back door are broken and French doors might be stiffer and easier to break by mistake."

Tyrell looks surprised, maybe by the fact that Em knows so well what the back of the house looks like. He raises his eyebrows at me, but I don't respond. She sees his eyebrows and gives a fidgety shrug. She looks annoyed at Tyrell. He sees her scowl and responds with a smile broad enough to show he's missing a molar or two on the sides.

"Front it is." I set my bag down on the porch, get a firm hold of the crowbar and start working it, trying to prise the big plywood board away from the door frame. I give it a good amount of muscle but nothing moves. Man, I nailed this sucker in real good. Tyrell and Em are standing next to each other on the front sidewalk, but they don't look at each other, and don't talk to each other either. There's a nervy silence behind me as I work. I am straining and get warm, sweaty, pretty quickly. Tyrell lights a cigarette, I can hear his thumb work the lighter, smell the dry smoke of his first exhale. No one talks. I start feeling foolish. Nothing moving, and the two of them just standing there like that watching me. So I stop. When I turn, I see Em scowling and Tyrell blowing a smoke ring in her direction.

"One of you want to give it a try?" I ask. I sound a bit annoyed myself. As I brandish the crowbar in their direction my phone starts chirping again. I ignore it, but it chirps and chirps. Tyrell looks at Em. Em doesn't look at him at all, but strides up the porch steps in her heavy boots and takes the crowbar from me.

"Why don't you answer your phone?" she asks, as I surrender the crowbar to her. But the phone stops just as she says that.

"Nah," I say "Nothing urgent." But then it starts ringing again. Dang that Peter is persistent. I feel myself getting all flustered, fumbly.

"Sounds persistent though." Em gets to work on the door. I raise my eyebrows at Tyrell and come down the steps towards him on the sidewalk.

"Hey."

"'S'OK if you need to get your phone." Tyrell says. Then he adds, with a grin, "I don't mind. I know how it is with a hot date sometimes." The dang thing is steadily chirping away. Peter clearly isn't leaving messages. He lets it ring until the voicemail kicks in and then he hangs up and redials. I should just shut the ringer off. I root the phone out of my pocket and try to shut off the ringer, but my hands are sweaty and heavy from messing with the crowbar and I accidentally answer it. I am holding it in the palm of my hand, and I can hear Peter's voice. When I look up, trying to decide what to do, wanting to fling the phone into the bushes or drop it and stamp on it, Tyrell just raises his eyebrows at me again, so I put the phone up to my ear and answer.

"Yes, Hello. Peter. Danny here."

Motherfucker, I can't get the board off the door either. I saw Danny struggling with it and I was sure I could do better. But I can't. The nails are in good and tight, and I can't get a good purchase—it's hard to even get the claws of the crowbar between the board and the door frame, and there's some sort of molding just under the board, some part of the door frame that keeps me from getting the claws far enough under to have any leverage. Danny's finally answered his phone. I wonder what all that's about. He looks jumpy as hell. And Tyrell. Why is Tyrell even here? Standing around smoking, blowing smoke rings at me. What the fuck? I'm shoving and struggling when he comes up behind me, wedges his smoke in the corner of his mouth and reaches for the crowbar:

"Miss Em. Let's try the French ones, alright? This one's not budging."

"Nah. It's OK. I've got it."

"Oh, OK."

I struggle with the door a bit longer, trying to ignore the smoke rings Tyrell's blowing towards me. After a few more tries with no progress, I stop.

"You're doing just great, Miss Em!" Tyrell quips. "Soon we'll have the whole *house* apart, am I right?" He's grinning hugely at me, cigarette balanced impossibly at the corner of his smile.

"Fine." I mutter, passing him the crowbar. "French doors. You try."

I can't imagine Tyrell's going to be right about this, but I follow him across the uneven floor of the old porch, taking my fleece off as I go and using its sleeves to knot it around my waist. He easily wedges the claw of the crowbar under the edge of the wide sheet of plywood across the French doors, and through his shirt I can see a surprising cut of well-defined, sinewy muscle. One good heave, his arms strong but wiry on the crowbar, and there's the satisfying creak of nails pulling up out of wood: the plywood starts to come away. Tyrell moves the crowbar methodically around the door frame, lifting the nails and bringing the plywood off. He's sweating by the time he's done, but his cigarette remains unbruised in the corner of his mouth: his capability makes Danny's efforts and mine look doubly ridiculous. He carefully lifts the plywood and props it against the wall next to the French doors. Once exposed, I can see the narrow pair of doors is pretty. Each door is comprised of rows of three small rectangular glass panes, maybe four or five rows of three, with a foot and a half of prettily molded solid wood at the bottom. The flaking white paint makes them look more charming, rather than less. They are lovely things: simple but of their time—I remember Danny told me the house was built in the twenties—and nicely proportioned.

"Uh oh," says Tyrell, seeing something he hadn't thought of now that he can actually see the doors themselves, "I'll bet these are dead-bolted top and bottom on the inside. Maybe we can't come this way after all."

I am too excited to slow down now. I just want to be inside the house. I grab a tarnished brass door knob and pull, hard. The door momentarily bows outwards and then there's the sound of old damp wood cracking and the bottom bolt gives: the door swings outward with the deadbolt rusted securely into the floor housing, and a mouse-sized piece of old water-rotten wood floor dragging along with it.

"Huh. Top bolt wasn't done." Tyrell says, but I am already moving past him, pulling the slim flashlight out of my pocket as I cross the threshold into the wet rot stink of Danny's Ma's house, hoping the rest of the floor isn't as rotten as this piece by the doors and being too keen to see inside to move carefully in case it is.

I have been arguing with Peter on the phone for several minutes when I see Tyrell and Em move over to try the French doors. My phone conversation has gotten louder but no more explicit. What isn't being said is that he needs my details so the scam can be laid on me: I *designed* the darned scam for them, and they should be happy enough with that. I don't want to take any rap should they be caught, dang it. I don't even know how they are making their illegal money. Guns? Drugs? Immigrants? I don't want to get nailed for something when I am not even in on the real substance of the crime, not to mention the significant profits.

"No, no, Peter. I am so sorry. I can't give you that right now. Try tomorrow OK? I know it is urgent. Yes. Of course. But I cannot. You are welcome to use my figurings without crediting me. No, I don't have a tax preparer's number either. No. It is not. No. Only for friends, Peter. I am sure you understand. You can tell the IRS they are your numbers, surely! I know you understand how those spreadsheets work, right? No, and I must really go. I am very busy this afternoon." On and on it goes.

I intend to tell Peter I am in the middle of a family emergency. I plan to tell him I am on my way to the hospital. I am just trying to concoct the right relative and an appropriate injury when I see Em yank a door open, loudly ripping something, breaking some part of Ma's house.

"Dang!" I yell inadvertently, and then with sincere urgency and perhaps the only honesty in the whole conversation: "I gotta go, Peter, man. Sorry!" and I hang up as I run up the front steps.

I push past Tyrell, not even listening to what he's saying about the doors, and I am in the front room, once the living room I'd guess. Once I am inside, my bad mood, my squabbling with Tyrell, recede. I am so glad to be inside the house. Just glad. Finally! I can tell I've got a big grin on my face. There's another dark room at the back, with no light coming in the boarded up windows. Kitchen is at the very back, I am guessing. I can see a room back there with a pale linoleum rather than wood floor, so that must be it.

Along the side of the house, on the same side as the front door we couldn't get open, is a wide entryway and a surprisingly broad flight of stairs: my flashlight picks out a simple wooden railing with nicely turned wood posts that fan out in a gracious curve where the bottom few steps widen. The balustrade is painted white and, like everything outside, it is flaking with disrepair. There's dark carpet on the living room floor. Wall to wall. And carpet sagging on the stairs too. Some of the little metal rods intended to hold it into the back corners of each step have popped out and lie askew on the treads.

I am compelled to go up, maybe by the fact that there's light upstairs because the windows are not boarded there? I don't know why exactly, I don't stop to think really, but I feel compelled; I head straight for the stairs, I want to go up. Tyrell and Danny are behind me but I am not listening to them. The stairs take my weight: the wood barely even creaks. I take them quickly, confidently, flashlight picking out my path, and then I am at the narrower upstairs hallway.

In front of me as I face the back of the house from the top of the steps, two open doorways into what look to be small bedrooms. The dusty windows let in grey afternoon light. I can see one window still has lace curtains hung alongside it. I can see the trees, mostly turned gold and red for fall, outside. I turn and to the side of the hall is a shut door with a glass knob. This is the door I want, though I can't think why; I can't make sense of the fact that having had nothing in mind, this is the door I was *looking* for.

I turn the knob but the door sticks. I turn it again and butt the door with my hip, hard, and it swings in on a large, square bathroom.

Oh. Here I am.

I take in a deep breath, like I could breathe in the whole space. Black and white tiles on the floor. This afternoon's light is dim, so the stained glass window doesn't tint the tiles, but I can imagine that brighter sunlight would. It's a peacock, the bird's body and head a royal blue, its tail feathers green and gold, fanning upwards to make a semi-circle. Against the same wall as the door I've come in, a sink and a foxed mirror. Under the window there's a big enamel claw-foot tub with a rust stain under where the spout must once have dripped.

I am breathing big gulps, like the first breaths one takes outside on a beautiful spring morning. Along the side wall between the sink and the tub, a toilet. Funny how that's never been in the dream. I am richly amused that the dreams have consistently omitted the scatological function so important in a bathroom. How polite of them, I think.

This is, of course, the room all my spinning dreams have been in, the room with the tired woman, the one in which I am just a small *boy*. It feels wonderful to be in this space, wondrous, like an epiphany. I walk into the room and spin with my arms outstretched: like in the spinning dream. Once I am spinning, I don't breathe anymore. I've already inhaled myself full, full of some feeling of completion. It's like a yoga breathing exercise, pranayama: I have breathed and now I retain the breath and feel everything within me, energy fizzing in my chest, down my arms and legs, like I could shoot light out of my fingers and toes. I stop and stand still, feeling a rare sensation of being in the right place. Spots of light come into my vision but I still feel elated at having found the room, like somehow the discovery will solve everything for me. I am going to pass out from the not breathing, but I want to pass out. It will be good to fall down here, to lie down here. I feel like here I can rejoin the dream and figure it out. I fall on my knees, one hand on the rim of the tub, which is where Danny catches up with me.

I can hear his voice climbing like frogs in his throat, upset with grief and panic. He's acting angry, but I can hear the frogs. "Out. Now!" he says sternly, grabbing me by the upper arm and trying to wrench me to standing. "Get out! Out of this room! You may not be in this room! Out, Out, Out, Out!"

DANNY

Em is fast moving into the house, and I don't make it to Tyrell and the open French door fast enough to stop her. I don't want her in there on her own. I should see it first. We should go together. But she is already in.

Tyrell gently nudges the broken deadbolt with the toe of his boot: "Oh, Danny. She's got some rot, this poor old thing." I look at the bolt, the broken bit of wood it wrenched up out of the floor, and nod wordlessly. Then I push past Tyrell into the darkness of Ma's living room and stand still a moment, trying to adjust my eyes to the lack of light. My flashlight is in my backpack, outside. I am not going back for it.

I strike a few steps towards the dining room and kitchen, the back of the house, before it sinks in that I can hear Em *upstairs*. Dang it! Already? She headed straight upstairs. I take the familiar-from-way-back-in-time stairs two at a time, and I know from the sounds in the floor, and just I already know: she is in the bathroom.

The door is open, and I can see in. In my chest, it feels like when music is really loud and forms a kind of invisible force, thumping your heart from outside your ribs. Seeing into that room is like meeting an approaching wall of loud, tragic Wagnerian opera, of all that happened *back then*. Solid, like getting hit, hard, in the middle of my chest. Like an invisible battering ram has swung out of that room and walloped me. But Em mustn't be in there. No no no no no.

I don't even know what I'm yelling but I'm yelling at her and trying to get her out of there and she won't budge. Why not? Why isn't she walking? Why is she on her knees? I'm yelling and dragging when Tyrell steps into the room, turns to face me, puts his hand on my chest and looks right at me, right into my eyes, like a grown-up trying to calm an irrational child:

"Whoa! OK, now. Danny! Let me help you. You take her under that arm and I'll take her under the other." He looks down, "OK, Miss Em? We'll find you a place to sit for a moment, catch your breath." Then to me "She looks like she's not well, Danny. Maybe not enough air. She needs a minute, OK? There someplace to sit in the front bedroom?"

I nod.

"OK then, Let's go."

It's easy enough to get Em standing, to start helping her shuffle carefully towards the front bedroom. My blood is rushing so hard I can hear it in my ears louder than any noises Tyrell or Em may be making.

I don't think there's anything left to sit on in Ma's old room but I let Tyrell lead us that way anyway. After she died I got rid of her matching wood dresser, armoire and mirror, her rose pink upholstered easy chair, the sagging mattress on its ancient springs covered with a throw that was supposed to look like a quilt but was actually just a white cotton blanket with a quilt pattern printed on it. She'd been in hospice for months when she died; no one had slept in that bed for a long time when I finally got rid of it. As we approach, I see the rose-patterned wall-paper (stained now but it cheered Ma up back then) dust, and buckled carpet. No furniture.

"Let's sit her on the floor? She can lean against a wall?" asks Tyrell.

I nod again.

We sit Em down and she smiles up at us. She looks pale, but happy. It's the first time I've looked at her face since coming upstairs. My heart's still pumping too hard from my own reaction to that room. It's the first time I look and there she is, *happy*, a beatific smile radiating from her like she's going to smile Tyrell and me along with her to the promised land. I am surprised. Again. Always with Em I am trying to figure out whether her reactions to my Ma's house should make me angry.

Tyrell nudges me "You brought cookies? Now might be a good time. And water? Can we open this here window, let in some air?" Hard to say if he's looking after Em by asking for the cookies or me: his tone is soft and placating. I get the sense he is giving me things to do to make me come back to my more normal self. I stand there just looking at him for a good while, and then I go to one of the windows that looks out over the street which, from this perch on the hill, looks surprisingly far below. The catch is stiff, but I can get it undone. The bottom pane slides upwards surprisingly easily.

"Good," says Tyrell, encouragingly. "Now, your bag, with the goodies?"

Em's got her arms propped out straight on her bent knees, her back against the wall, her head tipped slightly back and her eyes shut. She's still smiling. I turn and heavily, dreamily, thump my way back down the hall and the stairs, heading back outside.

My old and greying backpack is on the concrete walkway leading up to the house: it had made sense to leave it there when I was working the door open and we were all outside, but now it looks exposed and vulnerable. I am glad no passer-by snatched it. I crouch down next to it to do up the zipper, and just catch up with myself a little. I've got my head down, and my back to the road, but even so it's hard to ignore the conspicuously out of place shiny navy blue Prius that's driving down Alhambra far too slowly, fastidiously avoiding the puddles and the biggest of the lumps and bumps in the pavement. What the heck? I stand up slowly, carefully, like an invalid, and turn to face the car on the street just as its driver, a big woman with really short hair and a round face, lowers her window and yells over:

"Hey, I don't suppose you have my friend Em in there, do you?"

I am slow, out-of-it, and the whole afternoon is starting to feel like one weird bungled-up thing after another. I look at the woman in her nice car and just nod. I watch as she parks carefully on the street. I guess, thinking it through slowly, Em wanted someone here, just like I did: my Tyrell, her round-faced friend. When the woman gets out of her car and zaps the locks I see she's heavy-set but nimble. Jeans, plaid shirt, immaculately clean tan work boots.

"I'm Bev," she says, extending her hand to me as she gets up the hill. "Just thought I'd swing by 'cause Em said she'd be here."

I nod, say nothing, shake her hand and then I take her inside, pulling my flashlight out of my pack and lighting her way her upstairs to where Tyrell and Em are in Ma's bedroom, *laughing*.

When I get close enough to hear, I can hear Tyrell "Uh-huh. I see it! I see it! How about that one, over there? Looks like a pig with a little top hat on!" and they both laugh. Dang it. They are joking about the brown damp stains on the ceiling. I am irritated by how they are *not* taking this seriously.

"Em. Your friend is here."

I look up from where I am sitting on the floor in the front bedroom, and sure enough it is Bev.

I heave myself up and give her a hug. "Dude! Aren't you really early? We've hardly had a chance to look around yet!" I've caught my breath. I feel so happy to be here, but looking at Bev's wryly judgmental face, I realize that I don't want to try to explain about what happened in the bathroom. My euphoria. Maybe no one will mention it if I just keep moving along.

"Yeah, yeah. I was curious though." Bev looks at Tyrell "Any chance of a tour?"

"Oh, no. Ma'am." Tyrell gestures to Danny with an elaborate bow worthy of Shakespearian drama, "His house."

Danny looks like someone hit him between the eyes with a blow dart. He takes a deep inhale as if about to say something significant, and then his phone starts to ring, again, like it's been ringing all afternoon. He exhales, looks annoyed, then, quickly, like he's given up on controlling us all:

"You guys can all look around. But *not* the attic: those pull down stairs are not safe. Floors everywhere might have rot, so watch your step." He passes his flashlight to Tyrell: "Here."

Then Danny strides down the hall heading for the

stairs and as he makes his way back outside, I can hear him sounding angry as he answers his phone. Tyrell looks to me, then to Bev, then back again, and then gives a big shrug. "There goes our tour guide! Also, he took the cookies with him. I guess we'll have to take matters into our own hands."

Bev humphs, unimpressed.

"Oh, now. Wonders await, I'm sure!" Tyrell says to Bev, reaching out to pat her on the shoulder but then, mid-motion, changing his mind: he winds up flicking her shoulder with his middle finger instead, an unnatural gesture that looks like an affront although it has clearly come out of Tyrell's unexpected inability to follow through on his attempt at warm camaraderie in the face of Bev's disapproval. Bev just looks at him steadily, disparagingly.

"OK then! Ladies, if you will excuse me."

Once Tyrell has squeezed past us, I am left to balance Bev's sourness against my own immoderate delight. Keeping my tone cautious, neutral:

"Want to look around?"

"Yeah, sure. Em, what are you looking for here again?"

I am fake casual. I don't sound convincing even to myself: "I don't really know. I am just curious. I love these old houses and all the stories, ordinary stories you know, tied up in them. I just really like the look of this one."

Bev exaggerates her look around the dilapidated front

bedroom "Oh-*kay*" she quips. "Let's look."

We wander about in the two back rooms, both small, each with a pretty little window over the yard. I notice there's a big low circle cut in the plants, though it's still overgrown out there. It looks weird from up here, like someone was making a lunge-ring for a small pony. We look at the bathroom and I watch Bev expectantly as she walks into the room while I stay at the threshold, staying safe from the euphoria I feel in there. But it doesn't seem like she feels anything at all. She looks around, once, notes that the stained glass window is nice and then leaves, so I trail after her, disappointed in her lack of reaction, following her down the stairs and sharing my flashlight with her so we can peer into the kitchen with its big gaps where a fridge and a stove must once have stood, and its white counter. Single stainless sink, draining board. Doorway and steps leading down to the basement. Tyrell must be down there.

"Want to go down?" asks Bev.

"Nah." I want to be up, not down.

The dining room is just a claustrophobic closed room. It's hard to imagine anyone ever wanting to be in here. I wonder if it was one of those formal, awful dining rooms. I wonder if there were strained family meals here, if Danny's mother sat at the head of the table and silently glowered at Danny because he had dirty fingernails at the table. I wonder what they ate. Something with peas, surely, terrible greyish overcooked peas. Maybe it would be nice in there with the window unblocked, I muse, trying to be fair. Maybe with a nice table and a big vase of flowers on it.

The front room is much easier to be in. That is where I would have wanted to be, if I lived here as a child, I think. Right now it is maybe the most pleasant part of the downstairs because the open doors are letting in some light, and some air. There's a tangle of greenery out front, a bit of a vista because of the house's elevation: one can look out the doors and imagine green countryside or woods beyond rather than downtrodden urban housing.

Tyrell comes up the basement stairs carrying something. It bangs heavily against the walls as he lugs it, and then it catches hard on the doorframe as he tries to push through into the kitchen, nearly jarring him back down the stairs.

"Look what I found!" He sounds delighted, "Beauty of a wooden rocking horse! Real nice. I wonder if Danny knows he had it down there."

He sets it down in the kitchen and starts admiring it with Danny's flashlight.

DANNY

Phone. Again. When I answer it is David this time. Peter must have told him he was getting nowhere with me. I have much the same conversation with David that I had with Peter except I am angrier now because clearly, *clearly* even to them I am sure, I have something going on today and cannot deal with their problem. We talk around the subject, elliptically, elusively, for several minutes and finally I just give up. David, with a calm deep voice, is being authoritative: "So you see, Danny, we need . . ."

I move the receiver away from my ear and just hold the phone in my hand. I stand there looking at it, and then up at the house. I see the smoker across the street watching me and just stare, blankly I hope, back at her. I stand for a while. I can hear David "Danny? Danny are you there?" Then, phone in hand, I walk back into the house, into the front room and to the foot of the stairs. I hang up on David when I see everyone is in the kitchen looking at something by flashlight. I walk in and put the phone down on the counter.

"Oh. Linnie's horse." It was a gift from John, sent from a department store, ordered from overseas while he was deployed, and delivered with great fanfare. A poor choice: she was a newborn when it arrived. Then there was the fall. Linnie never rode it.

"It's a beaut, Danny!" Tyrell is so excited. "Nyasha's girls, they would *love* this! Or you should sell it. There's money in it. Vintage style. It's a real nice horse."

The big woman, Bev, and Em drift out of the kitchen and I can hear them pass through the dining room and back into the front room while Tyrell and I talk about the horse. He praises it, demonstrates how the action still works real nice despite its age. Points out how undamaged the finish is, how the paint still looks good. He loves it for those grandkids of his. So I offer it to him. He can have it. Don't know why I hung onto to it, frankly.

"Darned difficult thing to carry up the hill though, Tyrell." I joke, trying to be nice. "And I'm not helping!" I slap him on the shoulder, and walk into the dining room. From there I stand in the darkness looking towards the light in the front room.

I can see the falling-down that the darkness hid in other parts of the downstairs, the damp rot I had only smelled before. That faux-wood paneling from the early 70s is peeling from the walls now in long strips. The ceiling is dark with water stains, just like Ma's room upstairs. The once green carpet is moist, springy and black underfoot. There is a wooden dining chair with a broken leg and missing seat collapsed in the middle of the room under the spot where the ugly chandelier used to be and where three wires now protrude from the ceiling like branches growing down. I don't recognize that chair. I don't know who left it there. The smell of damp hangs thick in the air, the light from the window filtering through it. The street outside is quiet, though you can hear traffic on York like a far-off ocean. A big fly buzzes heavily in the overgrown ivy and weeds on the porch.

Em stands just to the side of the open doors, the shadow there seeming extra dark because she is beyond the rectangle of daylight. I can see her shape. I know she isn't wearing a skirt but the sweater tied around her waist looks like one in silhouette. She rocks very slightly side to side, but she has her back to me. I can't see her face; she seems to be looking out. Maybe her arms are crossed in front of her.

Then she starts humming. I recognize the tune. It is familiar, old, personal; something heavy and cold shifts in my stomach at its familiarity because it comes from my childhood.

A few lyrics mumbled out from her soft swaying: " Dream baby got me dreaming, Mmm, Hmm, Mmm, make me stop my dreamin' you can make my dreams come true."

Orbison. Dang it.

Dang.

My mother's favorite lullaby for me and then, years later, Linnie. I used to watch Ma stand in that window, rocking her skinny child as it tried to cry and sucked back its own slime and spit instead. Rocking, rocking, as if she could make it all right.

I wished I could make it right. The memory of my desire to help Ma keens in me.

She'd rub the little umlaut between Linnie's eyes and kiss her there and sing there in that doorway, just like that, and I would see how hopeless it was, how Linnie wasn't going to get better, how Ma was exhausted. I knew Linnie's illness was breaking Ma. I wanted, back then, so much to fix it. To make it better for Ma, because I had made it so terrible for Linnie.

"Sweet dreams, night time too," mumbles Em softly.

I can't stop watching, listening as the grey afternoon light makes that spot in the shadow blurry and makes it possible to imagine Ma standing just there, just like that, rocking and singing. That girl's wool hat in shadows looks just like Ma's hair wrap, her sweater like Ma's old skirt. I look at her for several moments, torn between the warm feeling at my heart at seeing what looks like Ma, Ma young and healthy, Ma before, and the dark fear feeling of remembering Linnie. Suddenly it is too much, too weird, Em looks too much like Ma. Why does Em know Orbison anyway?

"C'mon," I say loudly, accelerating carefully on the rotting carpet and making for the door. "Let's pack up in here, board her up and go home."

This whole day has been too much agitation. I can't think straight. The feeling I keep choking on is Linnie, the loss of Linnie. Grief. I want to cry it out. I want to be here alone and just cry it out. I don't want to be here with all of these people, and it is my house. If I say we go, we go, dang it. I am relieved to remember that it is, after all, my right to kick these people out. If I don't want them walking in my memories, I can ask them to leave.

I am so happy to be here, but the sudden activity preparing for departure leaves me confused. I wrack my brains to think of a reason to stay longer. Danny, on edge all afternoon, is so tense the muscles in his neck and at his jaw are visible, the ones at his jaw like mechanical nuts, as if his jaw is metal and the hardware is showing through his skin. He's bustling, getting Tyrell out onto the porch with the rocking horse, the rockers long enough that they are difficult to negotiate through any doorway, apparently. Bev is standing next to me, but she's got her iPhone out and is finger-swiping her way through the last hour or so of Facebook's offerings.

Danny interrupts her, calling from outside.

"Excuse me. Uh. . ." He's looking through the open door at Bev, clearly fumbling with what to call her. I imagine him calling her "Miss" or "Ma'am" and cough out a laugh. Bev shoots me a sideways glance, querying.

"Uh. Bev." Danny settles on keeping it simple, apparently. "Hey, Uh. Tyrell's got this rocking horse to take home. You mind giving him a ride?" Bev walks out onto the porch, and I trail after her. I run my fingers along the failing wood paneling, touching the house as I go. I don't want to leave. Bev stands there looking down at Tyrell, who's on the front lawn looking helpless as he clutches his awkwardly shaped, and, from the sag of him, apparently quite heavy wooden horse.

"If it'll fit, sure," says Bev. Tyrell looks pleased and concerned all at once. Bev turns to me and says quietly "You're going to have to come too. I don't want to deal with talking to him."

"Yes. Sure. *Oh!* The upstairs window needs shutting." I spin around to re-enter the house, glad to have a reason to go in one more time. I walk quickly through the living room, up the stairs and to the bathroom. I try the door: it needs a hip bump again. Then I stand in there and breathe, in out, in out.

"Em! C'mon. Let's go." Danny calls.

I start towards the stairs, and then remember the window I came up to close. It pulls down and latches easily.

By the time I am back outside, Danny's already shifting the boards back over to the French doors. I soon as I am out of his way he's nailing them back with a manic energy, jaw clenched hard. He must have brought nails with him. *Bang bang bang.* He's using far more than he needs, but they seem shorter, narrower than the nails we'd pried out earlier, more like nails you'd use inside to hang pictures on the walls than for big pieces of exterior carpentry.

"Hey, Em!" I startle, and look to see Bev is already down at the road with Tyrell, considering where to put the horse. "You got any string?"

I don't, but I know where Danny keeps it. I look to him but he's focused on nailing things down, so I just go round the side of the house, and sure enough, under the porch, obscured by some of the thorny bushes, there's the blue twine from the summer, neatly rolled and hung on a big fat nail, the kind of nail Danny *should* be using, I think to myself. I bring Bev the whole coil.

She's got the horse mostly in the trunk, with an old blue U-Haul blanket neatly wrapped around it to protect it. She deftly cuts a length off string with the little mother of pearl switchblade she keeps in her pocket, hands me back the remains, and begins securing the trunk low and tight to the protruding rockers.

Sideways, while reaching under the back bumper as she threads the twine through: "You ready to go?"

"Uh, yeah, I guess. I suppose. Let me say bye to Danny."

"No. He's coming too. I'll drive you all home." Bev says impatiently. "There's space."

"OK."

I get back up to the porch, and push through the bushes to rehang the twine on its nail. Danny has just finished his rather obsessive nailing down of the plywood. He's sweaty. He looks at me and nods.

"Bev's waiting."

"OK. You can go, Em."

"Nah. She wants to give you a ride too. She wants all of us in the car."

"Oh." Danny hesitates, looks around for his backpack, grabs it. "OK. Let's go."

I am surprised that he's willing to leave, just like that. I am surprised he doesn't want to look around more, check he's got everything. Say goodbye. Something. It's so quick. I am surprised he's willing to let Bev drive him back up the hill. I am busy being surprised as he walks away without a backward glance and for a moment I am on the porch all by myself.

Bye house. I think to myself, touching my fingertips to the porch railing. *Bye.* I ache inside. I am not ready to leave. I want more of that euphoria I felt in the bathroom. I want more. I want some sort of explanation.

Bye. Bye.

The dreams happen here, at this house. In my gut I have the feeling of unfinished business.

I walk down the front steps and confront Bev's Prius: Spotless, navy blue, Tyrell's horse sticking out of the trunk. Tyrell has seated himself in the front passenger seat. He makes a big show of rolling down his window with the automatic button, and then waves out at me. "Yo Miss Em! It's a *fancy* ride in here. I've got the seat warmer on!" Then, in a mock whisper "makes me feel like I'm wearing a freshly used diaper, if you know what I mean!"

Bev rolls her eyes. I get in the back. Danny, on the other side of the back bench seat, has his head tipped back, chin jutting towards the ceiling, and his eyes closed.

When it is done and each of the four is on their own again, they have time to feel.

The joker, thin and smiling, swathed in smoke rings, has his wooden horse, is full of delight: he has a gift to give, and feels with his whole soul the rightness of the gift, the uncomplicated pleasure of his being able to provide it to his grandchildren.

The cynic, bristly in her blue skydark car, is relieved: she does not have to be with the two men whose very masculinity unsettles her. She is worried about her friend, though this worry is assuaged somewhat by her friend's uncharacteristic serenity and happiness this fall afternoon. She feels compelled to clean her car, righting it to pristine condition in order that she may hide herself in it and feel as though she is in control in that most unsafe, most ungrounded of places.

The thin man is exhausted, his sinews strained, his stomach aching with a watery stew of new frustrations as they commingle with the weight of what is long past and long unresolved.

The walker is perplexed. Having reached a full place, she did not understand it; she found a locus and then left it once more.

In the Govans Urban Forest, the crows are beginning to come in to roost on the fall's gloaming light, in the ash trees, in the white and purple mulberries, in their exposed, bare branches. Crows and trees alike are silhouettes dark against a steely fall sky.

I know that walker and thin man are coming to each other, and to me.

The crows, black in the black tree branches, cackle news to the wind as the sky indigos itself towards nightfall, its pigment at this Hunter's moon clear like sapphire.

For the walker and the thin man, emptiness is receptiveness.

Now they are circuitry through which electric bright water, all experience, can flow.

They are watching, listening, waiting.

Now life can rush through without breaking them into pieces.

Now it is time for cataracts to rush fall tumble between the tall trees.

Tonight in the Urban Forest two young men, one blond, one dark of skin and hair, are finishing a long afternoon of work. Their footfalls are fleet, athletic. They wear their team jerseys: dark green with a slim white dog. All afternoon they have moved quick and spry on the serpentine of mulch laid in the tiny woods, pulling poison ivy, English ivy, kudzu—the so-called invasive species. They have been told to do this work, instructed that it is community service. Their hearts have profoundly different feelings about what they do.

The yellow haired, he speaks philosophically, has read, has felt even in himself, the power of the woods to uplift. He believes that there must be *pine groves, standing like temples.* He believes it is of service, is divine, to humans to let my trees give wonder. *The greatest wonder is that we can see these trees and not wonder more.* He believes there is uplift in the upgrowth of branches. In his heart he feels there is something more, of more good, to be received here under trees, even in a meager fraction of an abandoned and once decrepit city lot. *Nothing stands up more free from blame than a pine tree.*

His partner laughs on how these wondrous feelings have not been true to the history of his long past relatives, how trees were then not temples but gallows. Darkly he sings *Blood on the leaves/ Blood on the root* and feels bitterly about trees as only an escape from *Mount Misery,* a place to hide the *underground railroad,* a place to starve or hang. At work as the dark falls darker, he hurries to finish. There is a section of abandoned cement sewer pipe towards the back of the small wood, a crumpled blue tarp, and he wants not to imagine a human body hidden there, alive or dead. *Bodymore Murderland.*

The moon rises full, travel moon, dying moon, silver as a coin through the branches. She's the Grandmother Moon, Awenhai, Woman of the Sky who gives birth to all things, to the twins good and evil, to the everything

that connects these twins. She is old as all. In her face
the eternal, permanence.

Good and evil; twinned and twined; white and
black; owner and owned. How different the human
predicaments have been. How different when their
blood ran to my soil: home and horror.

Their ideas rush in parallel: different ideas on
different sides of a line.

The bags in the trees, the soda cups guttering from
moving cars: what am I if not the location of someone's
good luck, someone else's bad?

They are all of me, light and dark, living and dead.
They belong of me.
Not ownership, this, but a kinning, a right placement,
an embeddedness here.
I yearn for the equal opening to all of them who live
here through the soles of their feet to the force that flows
up from me to brightness.

Their differences, I knit together. I will it.

I knit the old twins good and evil together. I knit
the cruel and the kind, the lost the found, the pale the
dark the broken everywhen, while Awenhai watches. I
am this place. Lives mirror each other. The walker, the

thin man. Mirror lives along York Road, a seam, a join, a boundary that connects rather than divides.

I walk the dogs, just up Coldspring and back around Kerneway. Not far. It is already dark. I make myself a can of soup, New England clam chowder. It is comfortingly creamy but there's some preservative in there that I can feel on the sides of my tongue. I eat it on the couch with a messy handful of crackers while the dogs eagerly watch for falling crumbs. On Netflix I watch six episodes of *House Hunters International*, back to back. The show's formula (a pair of people who disagree about their budget travel to a difficult or glamorous new location to try and find a home, eventually reaching an uneasy compromise) is a reassuring anodyne, a comforting distraction, just enough to keep my mind inactive. I scratch the poison ivy rash a bit, idly, enjoying where my nails catch enough that clear yellowish fluid seeps up through my skin, a soft release. The dogs sprawl on the couch with me, enjoying my company, lazy. Then I go to bed.

I am not surprised when the spinning dream starts, after all I was at the house, in the bathroom, that very afternoon. I had found the dream's location. I am excited, expectant, and even happy to have the dream come back to me. Some of the day's elation and feeling of rightness tingles through me, but it quickly transforms into something else.

It all feels different this time, including my perspective.

As the spinning starts I feel out of control, and small. The bathroom, gold and blue light from the stained glass window, spins around me, whirling and tipping, and I can't breathe. I am choking on my own saliva, and then I am lifted into the bath, warm water in my ears.

The room spins. I can't see properly and the back of my head bangs hard against the enamel of the tub, again, and again. In the waking world I have never had a seizure, but in this dream world I know I am having one, and in this dream it is a familiar feeling. My muscles are rigid, contracted, and my limbs flail ineffectively. I can feel the tight curl of my wrists, my feet angling sharply, wrongly, in towards each other. Bones, head, banging the bathtub's walls and floors.

I shouldn't be seizing in the bathtub, surely. Water and snot in my nose and mouth, in my eyes. I can't see well. Then there above me, the shape of a boy, a young boy, his thin dark arms reaching to me, touching me between the eyebrows gently.

He rubs so gently there, but then shifts his hands to my shoulders and pushes me down into the water. I choke, swallowing.

Looking up I see the underside of the water as it flashes silver. There's great noisy thrashing because my body is still contorting itself.

The boy, I love the boy so much. He's got his face

turned away from the splashing and his eyes squinched shut. I want to tell him it is OK, I am OK. But I am not really OK. Neither is he. I try really hard to lie still and breathe the water in: I do it for him. The thrashing stops; it is like someone has turned off the motor in my limbs, taken the rigid arch out of my spine.

The room stops spinning and I can see his face looking at me as I look up through the wobbly, mercurial undersurface of the water. I am looking at his face and I love him, my big brother, and he loves me and I look at the golden and blue lights and then I let him go with my eyes, he lets me go.

I gasp in a huge breath of air and sit up in the dark of my bedroom on Kerneway Avenue. I am panting, terrified. *Shit.* The dogs startle awake and both look at me, worried, in the dark. *Shit, motherfucker, shit! I was just drowned.* I swing my legs off the bed, out from under the blankets, making Blue groan unhappily, and cradle my head in my hands. *Shit.*

After Bev drops me home, I go inside, dump my backpack by the front door and lie down on the couch. I mean to just rest for a few minutes, to pull myself together before the evening, but I fall asleep hard. I dream of Ma in hospice. She had a window by her bed in a room shared with three other ladies, all advanced care, beyond being able to toilet or feed themselves. All of them were "being kept comfortable" here, medicated out of pain and out of their minds in these last stages of their stubborn hanging on. I would sit on a little stool next to Ma's bed, hold her hand and watch out the window. From the fifth floor there was a nice enough view of tree branches.

Sometimes when I'd visit she'd seem lucid, and we'd talk about things. But then I'd come another day and she wouldn't even recognize me, or would be worried, obsessed about paying a bill when in fact that particular bill was a debt we'd paid off a year before. Sometimes she'd fuss about going out on some errand, something crucial at the pharmacy perhaps. Rather than tell her she couldn't go out, I would listen until she finished talking, and then ask if she wanted a cup of tea before her nap. She'd usually say yes, and then it would be like the very idea of going out had never been discussed.

In this dream, I am holding her hand. It is cold in

mine, the bones stand out, thin like chicken ribs under crepe-y skin. The knuckles are bulbous. Ma's hand. In the dream she asks what she never ever asked:

"Why, Danny?"

And in the dream, even though it makes me cry, I can answer her.

"She was too sick, Ma. It was killing you to try and keep her. And it was my fault in the first place."

Em walks in, wearing a white coat like a doctor, a stethoscope strung around her neck. In my dream this feels totally normal, appropriate. I am crying, tears running down my face. Em reaches over to take Ma's pulse, but then looks at me, puts the stethoscope against my shirt, over my heart and says,

"You know that's not true, Danny. You know Linnie was sick before she fell. She probably fell off the change table *because* she was having a seizure."

I'm weeping.

Ma is watching me sadly, but I can tell she doesn't know who I am anymore. She asks Em,

"Why is that man crying, dear?"

To which Em replies,

"He's waiting for you to forgive him."

"Oh. I can't do that, dear. I don't know him."

Then I see the little blonde boy hiding behind Em's back, his face peeking out from behind her hip. He's been there all along, and Ma, my Ma, reaches her arms out towards the child. He steps forward, a big smile revealing his teeth that look like white square pegs, and jumps happily towards her embrace.

A phone starts ringing and won't stop.

"You should answer your phone Danny," Em says. "Might be a hot date."

I wake. The room is filled with the silver light of the moon. Bright. Must be clear outside. Maybe a full moon. I rub my eyes, sit up. It is eleven according to the clock on the DVD player. I realize I left my phone on the kitchen counter at Ma's house, and looking at my backpack, slumped by the front door, I realize I also left the crowbar on the front porch. *Dang.* I hate carelessness like that in other people; I detest it in myself. I should go get the crowbar otherwise someone will break in. It's like leaving an invitation nailed to the door. Hey kids! Come drink your cheap liquor in here! And I should probably get my phone. I wonder how many times Peter and David called it? Hundreds probably. Battery must be long dead by now.

I get up and stare out the front window at Coldspring, the white moonlight making the street look oddly pale. Eleven. Kinda late to be out and about, but I want my phone and I should get the crowbar. I root around in my backpack to find my flashlight before remembering that I am going to have to take the plywood off again before entering the house and then nail it back on when I leave. Dang. That's a lot of work, and not easy work to do by flashlight. I should leave it for tomorrow. Well, I guess I could go remove the crowbar tonight at any rate and go back, *again*, in daylight tomorrow to open the place back up and get my phone. I sigh deeply, put on my coat, and head out.

There's no sleeping after the drowning dream. I can't shake the contradictory emotions of it. I can feel the water in my lungs, and feel my panic at dying. But I can also feel all that love between me and the boy, my brother, my brother who is Danny as a young child maybe seven or eight years old. Danny loved his sister, clearly, and she loved him. The chest-feeling is familiar to me: warm, like the way I love Will.

It's not that late, so I decide I'll walk the dogs. I think *I'll get some air* and then snicker at my own joke, for air is what I need most after my dream of water-filled lungs. It's late enough that the likelihood of my getting mugged seems unpleasantly high, but I decide I will take my chances. Blue and Girlfriend make me a difficult target, or at least I like to think they do. I haven't been mugged yet, but I keep waiting for it to happen. All the walking I do—it seems inevitable.

Girlfriend watches me pull on jeans and a sweater, and follows me downstairs when I go. Blue groans deeply and stays in bed. I have to call him down, and he thumps heavily down the steps as he comes, the look on his face clearly "but *why?* It is nice and warm in bed." I get harnesses on them both and we head out, down the road to Danny's Ma's house. It's bright out, a clear night and the moon is shining full. Not much traffic, just a few cars using the empty roads as an excuse to drive way too fast. I want to walk past Danny's Ma's house. Maybe seeing it will settle me down. I want to walk to think about the latest version of the dream. Was it a revelation or a baffling concoction of my own making staged in Danny's Ma's bathroom?

By the neon-bright bodega on the corner of York and Coldspring there're a couple of drunk guys talking loudly, leaning towards each other. I keep my head down and walk fast on the other side of the road, dogs close in at my heels. The men ignore me. I run to cross York, and for the rest of the way in the silvery light the walk down to the Alhambra house is easy, quick.

On Alhambra, there's a woman out smoking on her porch. She's in the dark, standing still. I smell her cigarette before I see her.

"Hey. ' Evening," I say I squeeze the dogs past on the narrow sidewalk between a parked SUV and the lattice that reaches down to the ground from her porch.

"You with the empty house?" she asks me, brusquely.

"Uh. Yeah. I guess."

"Kids got in there tonight."

I don't know what to say. Kids got in there *tonight* of all nights? Danny said he never got squatters. She flicks her cigarette butt off the porch and turns to go back inside before I can think what to ask.

The dogs and I cautiously, slowly, walk the last bit of the way, avoiding the puddles in the road. In the shadows thrown by streetlights, with the crispness added by moonlight, I can see that the plywood over the French doors has been pulled off, and that the doors have been broken too, glass shattered. Girlfriend starts straining forwards, yammering, pulling so hard in her harness that her front legs are off the ground, her head and nose reaching forward intently. Blue's got his hackles up, all in a ridge along his spine.

I'm scared as we approach. I am listening intently. Is there still anyone in the house? I get my phone out and turn the screen to flashlight, change my mind and set it to "911," ready to dial in case I need to. I tiptoe onto the porch, my breaths coming short and fast. The dogs, however, are noisily urgent: anyone in there listening would hear us coming. She said "got in", I keep thinking, "got" means they did it already. Does it imply they already left too? I struggle to hold the dogs behind me: I don't want them in the broken glass. I use my booted feet to sweep shards out of the way, swinging one leg then the other side to side. This too is loud. There is no hiding the fact that we are coming in.

Once the glass is somewhat clear, the dogs barge past me into the house, just like I barged past Tyrell earlier. They are barking and yipping, dragging me behind them. One of the nails from the cracked plywood—I knew they were too small and short to hold the plywood in well—catches my sweater and tears it as I get pulled through into the total darkness of downstairs. The dogs are being good scent hounds, excited by the darkness and intoxicated by some smell inside. I am reminded of old film footage of British people fox hunting, riding elegant horses behind a pack of barking hounds. I am not elegant, but my barking hounds on are on the scent of something. Through the living room they thunder. I am glad I know the layout of the place because down here at this hour without a flashlight you can't see anything.

Up the stairs we go, Girlfriend in the lead, still lunging along off her haunches and clucking, yipping as she goes, Blue barking in a steady baritone behind her. Upstairs, moonlight streams in through the back windows. I notice how different white light at night makes the place look; sunlight had been mellower, yellower. Now things look silvery, stark, unfamiliar. It's like looking at a photo negative, though no one takes photos on film anymore. In the hallway the trapdoor to the attic is open, gaping, and the pull down stairs are hanging askew from it, one side broken. I stumble on a bottle; that wasn't there before. Both are evidence of "the kids."

"Anyone here?" I yell, but there's no answer.

The dogs haul me onwards into Danny's Ma's room. It had been empty before but there are things in here now. Garbage. Boxes, maybe from the attic. Ripped open. It has a new smell of human pee in here. Did someone pee on the boxes? In the corners? The dogs are both barking now, until Girlfriend sets up howling.

She yanks me towards an overturned box, except when I look closer I can see it's a wooden crib on its side, an old fashioned one, low to the ground, like a manger or a small trough on wooden rockers. There's something next to it, inside a ripped open garbage bag. It is this that Girlfriend is howling over. It's hard to see in the moonlight, and as I bend to look, I reel with the possibility of what it is that I am half seeing. I see just enough to not want to see.

It doesn't smell bad, but I guess, if it is what I think it might be, it has been there for forty years now. I lean back, away, decide it must be a dead pet in the bag. It can't be that other thing. I pause for a moment, and then I lean back in to look, just to be sure and to confirm that the remains are innocuous, animal. However, what I see this second time is surely, undeniably, a small human skull, bones, the remnants, decomposed. I figure the "kids," whoever they were, must have come here looking to ransack the place, looking for treasures and mischief, and gotten this far. They found this carefully wrapped item and thought it was valuable, before opening it and realizing they'd found someone dead. That's what made them flee, I'd guess. And now I want to flee too. I want to pull the dogs away, the dogs making all of their racket.

I am dragging them hard towards the hall when I see a thin triangle of flashlight beaming up the stairs. *Shitshitshit.* There's no hiding me with my noisy dogs. My blood is rushing so hard it feels like I can't see or hear properly. Clumsily, I pull my phone out of my pocket and press the call button. It dials the 911 I've cued up and a woman's voice answers. I can faintly hear "Fire, Police or Ambulance?" over the dogs barking as the flashlight comes up the stairs and the moonlight reveals Danny's face.

"Jesus!" I double over with relief. "Danny!" I laugh. "Fuck! I thought you were a teenager with a gun coming to kill me." The dogs stop barking so much, both are wagging and hopping around, happy to see Danny, wanting to greet him. Cheerful idiots.

I watch Danny see me, I watch the confusion work his mouth into a strange grimace, and I watch his flashlight catch, first up, the open attic door, the broken hanging ladder, and then as he pushes past me into Ma's room, the crib, the ripped bag.

"Did you?" he asks, gasping, appalled, angry. "The *dogs*?"

"Oh, no! No, I didn't. The dogs didn't. We found it like this. Someone else got in here this evening. Broke in." Then, suddenly, I wonder why am I feeling guilty and catch Danny's arm.

"Dude!" I say, kind of joking. I am inadvertently echoing Bev's sarcastic and self-assured way of calling someone "Dude" when she really has in mind some unflattering thought about them. I look pointedly at the bag. He shakes me off, abrupt.

"Dude," I repeat, sternly this time. "Is that your sister

in there?"

He doesn't answer, but stands there, staring at me uncomprehendingly. In the relative quiet, I can hear the dispatcher at 911, still on the line. *Shit!*

"Hello?" I try to put the phone up to my ear just as Blue stumbles heavily forward towards Danny, yanking me along with him. "Hello? Sorry. False alarm." But there's no one there. I have accidentally hung up.

"Oh, shit." I say to Danny. "I called 911."

He looks at me, for a moment, stunned, and then he panics, starts walking in tight circles with his arms out, like he's looking for something to pick up, tidy away, but can't decide what: this empty bottle? This piece of plastic? Everything but the ripped-open black bag.

"I have to hide her before they get here."

"No. No. Let's just leave, Danny. Let's go. Now."

"No!" He's crying-yelling, spinning in circles now. It's like watching the dream spinning but in the dark, and from the outside. "Oh, no! No, no, no. Em, Em. They will put me in prison for it."

I am thinking quickly, adrenaline pumping, "Danny, you were just a kid. It was *mostly* an accident. Plus I bet cause of death isn't even clear anymore. You could say your Ma did it. She's dead; no harm done if you blame her."

Danny gawps at me. "*How . . . ?*"

"I don't know. I *know*, Ok? I think. Something. I know something, maybe. It doesn't matter." *Of course it matters.*

Sirens are coming. They always make Girlfriend howl and tonight is no exception. She echoes their every wail with a wail of her own.

"Let's go."

Danny leads the way down the stairs, and I stumble along behind the dogs after him.

I feel like someone poured white Elmer's school glue in my ears: my hearing is muffled, my heartbeat louder than anything else but even it seems like maybe it's coming from somewhere other than me. I can't think. The moonlight makes everything seem like it is in an old movie, black and white, as if I am watching something that happened to someone else. Em is on the stairs behind me, and her dogs are a happy bustling mess between the two of us. I worry they are going to shove past me on the stairs, trip me. Between them, the darkness and the loose carpet, it feels treacherous.

By the time we get into the dark of the living room, I can hear that the sirens are passing on York Road: these ones are not coming for us. They are on their way to some other calamity. That's good. I try to breathe a little. As I get to the French doors, which are all broken up, I look for something to batter the jagged edges with a bit more: it's dangerous all the shards and nails in the dark. It would be good to make it smoother. There's no sign of the crowbar. Maybe it's inside in the dark somewhere. Maybe the intruders (why does Em feel so sure it was kids?) took it with them. It's a useful item. There's nothing to make the doors better just now, so I warn Em.

"Watch yourself coming through" I say, "And your

dogs too."

"Yep." Em replies. "I know" and she reaches forwards past me to finger a bit of cloth stuck to a nail before reaching back to show me the hole it left at her shoulder. We squeeze through carefully. The dogs are a big panting tangle, oblivious. I hope they are OK. They are not complaining if they did get hurt.

Then we are on the porch, in the bright of the big full moon, and I don't know what to say, so I just stand there, looking down on the street, seeing the moon mirrored in the big puddle out there.

Em clears her throat. "I, Uh." And she stops. "Ah."

I say nothing. My thoughts stay glued together. It's like if I unstick them all the panic will come flooding between them and I will be the one drowning.

In not thinking, trying not to think, trying not, all the thoughts clump and braid into each other so that I am repeating, circling, breaking into and out of all these sticky strands: Someone knows.

How. How does she know? How could she possibly? Guilty thoughts.

Does she know how Ma walked in and found me? Does she know that Ma pulled the baby out of the tub, a wave of water coming out with her, that Ma shook her, yelling her name and trying to do CPR? That eventually, sweaty with effort, she gave up, and left Linnie on the floor, with me curled up fetal next to her in the puddle of cooled bathwater, that she stood with her hands on the rim of the sink weeping, retching up bile, weeping more and then finally just standing there still and silent, looking at herself in the mirror?

We hid Linnie in the attic so that social services would leave Ma alone. We put her in layer after layer of black garbage bag. We scotch-taped it all shut. We put her in the old crib and put the old crib up in the attic. Up high. People look for bodies down low. We thought we were being clever, hiding her up high in the air. Taking advantage of his absence and confident John wouldn't ever *talk* to the neighbors or what few acquaintances we had, we told people that John's mother in North Carolina had taken the baby because she would be able to care for her full time. We banked on the fact that no one knew John's last name, and that his mother was long since dead. One time squirrels got in the attic and we panicked that they'd get into the bundle, chew holes, but I put poison up there and nailed extra boards and chicken wire over all the little gaps, and a sturdy grate over the vent.

I am willing myself to stay glued shut. I don't even realize I am crying until Em touches me, puts a hand up to my face and her fingers come away glistening in the weird light of the moon.

Somewhere, a phone rings.

It's my phone, on the counter in the kitchen. It's probably Peter, or David, *again*. The absurdity of it makes me start to laugh.

"Hot date?" asks Em, somehow picking up Tyrell's joke from earlier and weirdly echoing her comment in my dream from just an hour or so ago.

"Mighty fine phone battery!" I cough out, "Been testing it all day."

Then I am laughing and crying at the same time as the phone rings back in Ma's dark kitchen. Em's dogs start whining and trying to pull in circles as I laugh harder and harder. My laughing feels good. It makes Em laugh too. We are both laughing hard, loud, so it takes a while to realize that the dogs are starting to act crazy, feral. I see Em look to them. The little one's eye whites are showing and she is frantic, trying to pull off the porch. The big one's got his tail tucked under and his hips rounded down. I stop laughing abruptly.

"What's up?" I ask Em.

"Dunno. My dogs never act like this. 'S weird." She lets the little one drag her and the other dog towards the stairs down to the sidewalk.

"Coming? Maybe they know something we don't."

"Huh. They must not like it when I laugh!" I try to joke, but the dogs are pulling Em hard, so I follow. They pull so much she trips on the steps and falls, missing a step or two to land solidly on her knees on the sidewalk at the road. That must have hurt, landing like that on the concrete. I grab her by the upper arm, help her up and as we are both righting up to standing we are facing the street and the puddle. Except it's not a puddle anymore.

Its surface is welted with dark water boiling up quickly from somewhere underground. It's getting bigger and wilder real quick. There's a lot of water coming up fast.

"Oh, *dang*. That's not good. Let's hustle, Miss Em!" The dogs are keen to run, and I've got Em by the upper arm as we run and limp up Alhambra towards Winston, getting to higher ground by standing on the steps of a neighbor's house across the street some five or six houses along. The streetlights and the moonlight show the shiny dark welter of a puddle spreading still, waves and bubbles erupting from it in multiple places. Em is leaning down to look at her knees, which seem from the darkness on her jeans to be bleeding.

Then there are sirens again, coming from Beaumont, heading towards us. The dogs are silent this time. When I look down I see the big one is shivering hard with fear. His teeth chatter so loud I can hear them in spite of all the other noise. Two firetrucks are bearing down on us, lights flashing, sirens wailing.

As they get closer, there's a wet sound, sucking, like a child eating soup noodles, from the road where the puddle is. The water is subsiding and, in chunks with jagged angles, parts of the tarmac are too. Wet sounds. Then the earth starts to fall away, the road folding in on itself and falling down. There's a deep hole. In the moonlight, even with street-lights, I can't see the bottom. It's a really deep hole. I can hear the firemen yelling *Back it up! Back it up!* And I start laughing again. With the sirens still going, they sound like a dancehall rap mix, the MC calling out moves for the dancers. The trucks are reversing; the hole is getting bigger. A big piece of Ma's sidewalk falls into the hole with white and red flashing lights from the trucks lighting its way. The night air smells like wet clay infused with sewage.

Then there is groaning and creaking and loud snapping from Ma's house as the hill, with the house on it, starts to lean towards Alhambra. The house and the hill are both then leaning like the Tower of Pisa, impossibly far, until the most possible impossible thing happens: The house, the hill, the last bits of sidewalk, all slide sideways, crunching and groaning, like they are going down a massive escalator, into what becomes an implausibly deep, improbably circular sinkhole.

I think, unexpectedly, now of all times as the world is falling into a hole, of Mr. Willis, my history teacher when I was seventeen. He was British originally, and in Baltimore somehow because of his American wife, I don't remember why. He had a habit of detouring from Roland Park Country School's intended curriculum, to correct, he said, our xenophobic American educations. He wanted us to know how the world was inter-connected; he wanted us to see how an event in one place had repercussions in another.

He wanted us to see that though there were trends in human history (*The Rise and Fall of the Great Empires*, for instance), the earth itself, with its volcanic core, tectonic flexibility, and meteorological force, could unsettle everything and surprise us. Cataclysmic change could, and often did, come from below in the shape of earthquakes and volcanoes, or from above in that of storms.

Though a historian, Mr. Willis also blew our minds telling us about Boltzmann, the philosopher-mathematician, who argued that what we think of as predictable is actually just probable. Things tend to follow the most likely course. Heat flows to cold simply because that is the most likely thing for it to do. Likeliness is no guarantee though: the unlikely can and does still happen too, now and again.

Mr. Willis had floppy hair, British hair, longer than American men's hair. He wore skinny leather ties (black, white and sometimes even patterned) with his pastel-colored dress shirts. He would orate his digressions, half acting them out. As Danny's Ma's house fell into a hole, I thought of his rendition of Thomas Stamford Raffles, a more famous person than I, confronting a geological improbability some two hundred years ago:

Raffles, Governor of Java, was waiting for the sun to go down enough that he could indulge in his sundowner, the stiff gin and tonic he had looked forward to all sweaty afternoon, the drink that would ease his concerns that he still, even after four years, understood so little about Indonesia. His Malay stood him in good stead, certainly, but all those islands, and Dutch-French history to boot! He was rubbing the back of his sunburnt and sweaty neck, running a finger under his tight and stiff white collar to give himself ease when he heard the cannon fire: close, too close. But where exactly? It was days before the story finally became clear, clearer, amidst the thickening ashclouds of what burgeoned into two full weeks of volcanic eruption: what he had heard was in fact not cannon fire from a too-close ship, but the explosion of Gunung Tambora on Sumbawa eight hundred miles away.

At first it was beautiful. Around the world, the sunsets were golden and pink (Turner would paint them over and over in following decades), but then the sky wouldn't clear and the temperature fell just enough to ruin the crops. As the months of grey sky went by, people became hungry.

The ash drifted North and South. In England, the following year was the year of no summer. There was famine. The Irish lost their potato crops. Because their rice wouldn't grow, the Chinese planted the hardy opium which would ultimately undo them. The rains brought typhus and new strains of cholera evolved.

Schubert wrote about winter, Byron wrote about darkness, and Mary Shelley created Frankenstein's creature.

The summer didn't come. The crops didn't grow. The people were hungry and diseased, all because of Mount Tambora, Indonesia.

A volcano meant the summer didn't come, *at all*. At seventeen, seeing Mr. Willis pantomime his way from Raffles to Frankenstein's monster, I couldn't imagine how people kept on going. Having seen that summer did not actually come one year, how did they convince themselves that it would ever come again? At seventeen, I thought I would have just given up and died.

A volcano, a sinkhole. Who ever really knows what's going to happen?

Raffles went to Singapore from Java. There a famous hotel was named after him. In that hotel the world's most famous drink, the Singapore Sling, was concocted about a hundred years later. A gin drink: Raffles would have liked it.

The police arrive at Alhambra Ave., cruisers with their lights flashing like colored strobes lighting up the people that are emerging from their houses into the moonlit dark to see what the hell is going on out here. The house next door to the space where Danny's Ma's used to stand is a long, low, blue bungalow: its south-most wall leans to the side, towards the big hole, but it doesn't fall in. There weren't any cars parked on this particular stretch of Alhambra, but some of the emerging people are moving their cars further out of the way, just in case, reversing up and away from all that has sunk down.

Firemen with yellow tape, arms outstretched, yelling against all the various kinds of noise (cars, sirens, grumbling rocks in the earth) are trying to get people out of the immediate area. They are trying to rope off the big hole, to get us all back from it. The light is surreal: moonlight and red, white, blue flashing. It makes the strange scene even stranger. This couldn't possibly be happening. But it is.

Danny and I are ushered further along the street. I see the woman who had been on her porch earlier this evening, the smoker who had warned me about kids having gotten into the house. Her shiny black skull cap glistens when the swirling lights hit it:

"You Jojo's boy?" she asks Danny.

"Yeah." He doesn't even sound surprised she's asking. I am surprised. She *knows* him?

"We was in school together. Grade one, maybe. Why'd you stop coming?"

"Oh," says Danny "Yeah. Of course." Then, "Followed my Step-Dad. I went over with him. Lived on base," as though distracted, as though he doesn't really care what he says to this woman from his past, and totally nonchalant about the time he's skipping over when he must have been here, but just messed up and not attending school.

"Hmm." The woman says, skeptical, looking at me as though I have something to do with it. Then back to Danny: "You was cute back then. Big eyes. You used to skateboard down this hill."

Danny smiles ruefully: "Yeah."

"What happened to your sister? I remember social workers poking around asking if you was all beating on her over there."

"We weren't. She was sick, it turned out. She died. Back in North Carolina," he says, confidently, and then, without further explanation, turns from her to me, and puts a hand to my back to direct me up the hill towards one of the ambulances crowding the area behind the firetrucks.

"*Miss Em*, get these folks to look at your knees" he says, with exaggerated politeness, reaching to take tangled leather out of my hands, "I've got the dogs."

Danny

The funk, mud, sewage smell just gets worse as time goes on. Em's dogs don't like seeing her walk away. The big one cries like a whale singing and the little one sets up a steady rhythmic yap until I tap her muzzle with my fingers. I don't want to talk to that neighbor woman again, so I move off slightly up Winston. My impulse is to walk away. I feel like maybe it can't touch me anymore, can't harm me . . . even though I know the hard evidence is still in that deep hole. The hill gives me a bit of a view over the chasm where Ma's house used to stand. Seeing how truly *gone* the whole house is, and how the hole looks like a huge well, an exaggerated elevator shaft, a tunnel dug by a giant, I cough out a laugh which startles the dogs.

I wonder if all this means I am off the hook. Can I just let all my guilt fall down the hole? I feel shocked, in limbo, but already this possibility is tantalizing. What about Em's *knowing*? How could she? I can't figure this and I know she's not after harming me, so I let the thought drop. I feel good: rattled, jittery but optimistic, like I am falling into a pit of relief I think and then I laugh again. Can one fall down into a good feeling?

Will the bones be salvageable? Maybe, and with DNA testing these days maybe it'd be easy, if the forensics on TV are right, for the police to track who they belonged to. But the layers of plastic are ripped open which will let in decomposition as well as squirrels and rats, and everything is down in that deep, muddy, watery hole. Maybe no one will ever find anything? All that water, that dark force that was rushing around up here is now rushing around down there, moving things, surely, taking it all apart? What's happening in that hole? Maybe it is still going, down all the way to lava?

I am standing and looking, avoiding making eye contact with people as the area gets more crowded with onlookers. The dogs give me an excuse to keep shifting out of the flow of human traffic. I hear people asking each other questions about who owned the house that disappeared and I am glad they don't know it's me.

There's something like a parade about this, a street festival. I remember walking up York Road once, right into a marching band parade and having no idea what it was for, the dancing and music, the women in pink satin outfits with feathered headdresses.

I feel like that now: I am at a celebration, a noisy festive one, and I don't know what it is for. I feel like dancing. I want someone to bring out the marching band. I want this to be New Orleans carnival! I want to hear trombones and drums celebrating the past that has been washed under, to hear the brass call for a strong future in spite of what has been lost. I start dancing a bit in spite of the lack of music, just a step or two side to side. The dogs, Blue and Girlfriend she calls them, get excited. I yowl "whoo-ee!" and it makes the big one, Blue, start barking and panting, mouth open like a dog-smile. The little one is spinning in circles. We are becoming a big happy tangle.

I am surprised when two young white guys in wife beater shirts and shiny basketball shorts emerge from the house a few doors along from Ma's, ushered out by a pair of nervous and urgent-looking law enforcement officers. Who knew those guys lived there? Took *them* a long time to realize the ground was falling beneath their feet. They must be solid sleepers to have missed all of this ruckus.

When Em comes up to meet us again the dogs are extra happy, jumping and bouncing and whining. She is wearing shorts! Her jeans are cut to the mid-thigh like old-lady shorts you'd buy at Walmart.

"Paramedics amputated the legs of my favorite jeans!" she exclaims.

I laugh, and hug her, pass her the dogs, and dance in a little circle, my arms raised high, twirling hands, now that I don't have to hold the dogs any longer.

Both her knees have big white gauze pads taped to them, and those rectangles seem to glow in the moonlight, streetlight and emergency lights. In the strobe-like swirl of lights, I can't tell whether there's some kind of livid rash on her shins or if they are streaked with blood from her knees. It looks bad.

"Painful?" I ask, still dancing and slightly concerned

that it may be callous of me to be so carnivalesque if Em is in real pain.

"Yes! But not really. It's nothing, really. Nothing a little cleaning and antiseptic couldn't fix." Em laughs at my dancing, pauses, and then "You going to tell someone it's your Ma's house?"

"Nah. They'll find me eventually. Property records and all that."

"Guess you really missed your hot date's call now, huh?" Em smiles. "Sorry about your phone."

Ha! My phone. Dang it that's *also* mighty fine. I'd rather not have a phone than have Peter and David implicating me. I smile at Em. I feel light and airy in my lungs, like all the flashing light in the darkness is somehow sparkling off my teeth. This whole thing can make a fresh start for me.

I stretch, hands in my low back, arching side to side, and then stand straight as I can and resolve to myself: no more crooked numbers, no more guilt about Linnie. Fresh. I start dancing again, round in a circle. Em follows me for a couple rotations, stiff and awkward with her padded knees and her huffing, happy dogs. She's laughing and I am hooting, almost uncontrollably "Whoop! Whoop! Whoop!"

It must be several minutes before I stop.

Em looks at me and smiles.

I smile back, big as I can, showing all my old stained teeth as though they are bright and radiant.

"Walk you home?"

"Yep. Sure."

She's awkward on her sore legs, a bit unsteady, and the dogs are excited, pulling hard and sweeping round back behind her, tangling and then shooting forwards ahead again. She looks like she's having trouble. I reach out for the leashes. She looks at me, smiles again, untangles the dogs and passes them off.

"Am I speaking with Emma Fletcher?"

Groggy, I am clutching the phone, confused. I fell asleep hard after I got home. It must be five or six judging by the light: close to dawn. I'm struggling to sit upright, awkward with one hand clutching the phone to my ear and the other trying to free my knees from under the covers so I can sit. They are stiff. They hurt.

"Yeah." I am finally up and seated, and can now scrabble at the lamp trying to find the switch. I turn the lamp on, and then have to clumsily recoil from it because the light is so bright it makes my eyes hurt and water.

"Yeah. *Yes*. Yes. Sorry. I am Em Fletcher. Speaking."

"Ms. Fletcher, William Peterson has given you as his emergency contact. What is your relation to him?"

"Will's my brother. *Half*-brother. Same Mom. We have different last names." I am struggling to wake up, to move past the all-consuming sinking of Danny's house, to absorb and process what is currently happening. Confoundingly, it seems to have nothing to do with last night. It feels like *everything* should have to do with last night, and the amazing spectacle of the house sinking.

"What's going on? Who am I speaking with?" I ask, trying to think of Will.

"I am calling from Surrey Memorial Hospital. We

have William Peterson here in acute psychiatric care."

Surrey Memorial is a ten story building on a triangle of land between on on-ramp for the beltway and an off ramp for the I-70. The building's exterior is teal glass panels. In the morning sun, light glints off them sharply. On my first approach, I can't figure out how to get to the building or get into the parking garage and wind up on I-70, speeding towards Columbia and Ellicott City, cursing. The detour costs me time. It is seven-thirty and fully morning by the time I find my way back, find the right exit, find my way into the parking garage and figure out whether to take the ticket automatically issued to me at the garage's entrance gate with me or not.

In the lobby, I ask Vanessa, an "information consultant" according to her badge, how to get to acute psychiatric care and she directs me, listlessly to floor four. "Bad Feng Shui," I quip and she just looks at me.

"'Four' sounds like the word 'death' in Cantonese," I add. "It's bad luck."

Vanessa looks steadily at me, and then pointedly turns her attention to the candy crush game she's playing on her cell phone.

I take the elevator. On the fourth floor, its doors open onto a security gate like airports have: there's a scanner portal to walk through and two security guards with metal detector wands.

"Ma'am," says one of the guards, walking towards me

quickly "You on the right floor?"

"Four?" I ask, once again confused and uncertain. "I'm looking for a patient in acute psychiatric care? Will Peterson?"

"Wait there, please." One guard, the bald one, stays, watching me. The other, with hair and a beard too, disappears behind the security apparatus. When the beard returns he has a clipboard with him that he hands to me: "Fill this out please. Visiting doesn't start until ten. Fill this out and wait. I'd recommend waiting in the cafeteria on level B as we do not have a lounge."

I have been nodding, apparently listening, but it feels like nothing is going in.

"Is my brother ok?" I ask.

"I am not a medical professional, Ma'am," says the bearded officer. "Please fill out the form."

There is nowhere to sit, so I stand with the clipboard. The form is, it turns out, a combination of rules for visitors to acute psychiatric care and a liability waiver absolving Surrey Memorial in the event that I am attacked by a patient or otherwise injured while I am here.

The list of prohibited items includes what I suppose are common sense items to not bring to, what is this place? A prison? I remember urban legends about the superhuman strength of the mentally ill, men ripping off their own arms, or escaping the clutches of multiple nurses. I hadn't thought about it before, but of course,

I suppose, one doesn't want anything flammable, or firearms, or knives. I am surprised by the explicit prohibition of hoodies, high-heeled shoes, necklaces, hoop-earrings, eyeglasses, sunglasses, wallets, cell-phones, scarves, pens, pencils, plastic cutlery and keys (these items can be left, at your own risk, with security).

I fill in the form, sign it, and pass the clip board and pen to the bald officer. Then I hobble, sore-kneed, back to the elevator, and to my car—passing Vanessa (dozing) in the lobby en route—to drop off my belt, sunglasses, and the leather bracelet with one Ghanaian trade bead on it which I wear to remind myself that once I travelled. I leave my cell phone in my glove compartment after wishing for a moment that I could call Danny and find out how he is this morning but I can't. First, I've never had his phone number and second his phone is now in a sinkhole with his Ma's house and everything else.

I make my way back to the main building, glare at Vanessa (still dozing) as I pass through the lobby (surely she could have spared me some of this painful to and fro?) and head to the cafeteria. Here the elevator doors open to a palpable aroma of scrambled eggs and oatmeal. I sit at a sticky white table in the windowless room reading, back to front and then over again, a left-behind copy of yesterday's *Baltimore Sun* while drinking tepid Red Rose tea out of a small styrofoam cup.

Just before ten, I head back upstairs. The bald guard and the bearded one frisk me, take and catalogue my car keys, and send me through the scanner. Then I wait outside a windowless door which requires a key-swipe to open, and which has a blue button next to it: "Press <u>ONCE</u> for nurse," "once" underlined emphatically. I press the button, and wait, for a long time. I'm nervous, and worried about Will. I want to press again. What if no one heard the first time? It is *very* tempting to press again. I look at the underlined "once" and make myself wait. I stand still. I feel the scabs on my knees getting stiffer. I have no phone, no watch, and there is no clock on the wall. I wait.

I am startled out of a state of stultified anxiety when a male nurse bursts abruptly through the door: blond, young, well-muscled, blue-eyes, immaculate American smile. "Hi. I am Adam. Who are you here to visit?"

"Will Peterson?"

"OK, yep. He's stable. You can come with me."

Adam leads me down a hall that initially seems like any other hospital hallway: gleaming floors, putty-white walls. However, perhaps because of the daunting list of prohibited items I had to sign off on, I notice the absence of things. There are no curtains, no chairs, no gurneys in the hall, no alcoves with a spare wheelchair or two, no files, no paperwork, no place for such things.

In a completely unadorned room, on his own, with a high window that looks like it is made out of some especially thick plastic, the kind you'd see protecting the crowd in an ice-hockey arena, is Will, on a bed with no blanket, in a hospital gown, asleep. His mouth is slightly open.

I don't understand, and I am fighting down panic as I ask Adam "Why is he here? Is he OK?" and, drawing only on movies and horror flicks with psych-ward settings, "Has he been drugged with something? Is he violent? Can I wake him?"

With a start I realize it's been less than twenty-four hours since I last saw Will: "I just saw him yesterday and he was OK!" But even as I say it, I remember that Will wasn't really OK yesterday, that he was bruised and beaten.

Adam smiles, reassuringly. "Let him sleep for now. I don't really know about anything except that we did give him a sedative. I'll get the attending to come talk to you, alright?"

Adam leaves and I stand there, looking at Will. He looks much cleaner today, like maybe they washed him. Certainly his face is free of grime and snot. His feet are pink and shining. They look healthy. I can't remember when I last saw Will's naked feet. His fingernails are still rimmed with grime, but otherwise he looks fresh, relaxed. That one eye that had been swollen shut when I last saw him looks a bit better, but I notice it is still weeping, tearing a bit, even as he sleeps.

The attending is a brisk woman in her thirties with no time for me. She barely looks at me as she walks in and announces that she will summarize the police report:

Will showed up at someone's house in Timonium last night, someone who didn't know Will or vice versa. The front door was unlocked and he didn't knock. He just let himself in and sat down on the couch in the living room with the resident's two teenage children who were at that time watching TV. The woman of the house thought he was deranged and didn't know what to do. He said "Merry Christmas!" to her and asked for a cup of tea with milk, which she made for him and he drank while watching TV. She called the police shortly before eleven p.m.. Before the police arrived, Will had gone to the kitchen and washed his mug, as well as some of the family's dinner dishes, by hand, not loading the dishwasher. He repeatedly said "Merry Christmas!" and laughed. He called the officers who arrived on the scene "Santa's little helpers." He was taken into police custody at eleven forty-eight p.m.. He was admitted to the acute psychiatric floor at two twenty a.m.. He has been given tranquilizers.

Danny

It took a long time for me to fall asleep tonight, until almost dawn really, after all the excitement, the festival of the day. My nerves were over-done and jangly. Eventually, when I did *finally* fall asleep, it was fitful and I had one dream after another, always of the house, always of looking for something. It felt like I was working really hard while sleeping, or working really hard to be asleep, or some combination of the two.

Then I have this different dream: I am in Ma's bathroom, the peacock window shining warm light, gold, blue and green on the floor tiles. Em is standing at the sink, her hands on the rim; I can see her reflected in the mirror that hangs there. She's got her eyes shut, her face tipped downwards. There's water running in the sink, gushing. It is rusty-colored, like it has soil in it, like the water looks after the city has been working on the mains, tinted orange by the heavy clay in the orange soil outside. There's water running in the bath too, also rusty-dirty. In the bath the water is draining so fast there's a whirlpool. A big whirlpool. Too big. It touches the enamel of the tub's walls, sucking fiercely and noisily downwards. I put my hand in the tub's whirl and it feels like my fingers being licked by Em's dogs, warm, muscular, and oddly reassuring.

That is the last dream of the night, I decide.

I get up; it is eight forty-two a.m. which is early for me, and especially early after all last night's late-night drama. I feel pretty happy about life.

I make tea. I look for the file of documents I have for Ma's house and find it on the top shelf of my closet, next to the sweaters I never wear because they itch. I'll have to call the city, or maybe the police. Probably both. I have no phone.

It's Monday. I watch bad TV all morning.

I make and eat a bologna sandwich for lunch.

Then, though I don't know if Tyrell will be around, I walk over to his house on York. I knock and wait awhile; he meets me at the door.

"Hey, man. Afternoon!" I hug him and then: "Got time for a walk? I want to show you something."

Tyrell is puzzled. "Where?"

"Back at Ma's."

"OK" Tyrell raises his eyebrows, and scrunches up his mouth: genuine and mock curiosity all at once. "Let me grab my keys."

We cut down through Wilson Park, across Coldspring and up Ivanhoe to get to Alhambra: I am a little cunning in choosing this route as it is both a way to walk from Tyrell's house to Ma's while avoiding a lot of the traffic *and* a way to walk there with no clear sightlines until we are basically right at the cordoned off area. I am delighted with the effect of my plan: Tyrell is telling me how annoyed Nyasha was yesterday about him skipping out of Church early to come with me. He's describing the phone message she left for him, reprimanding him, as he turns the corner onto Alhambra and stops, mid word.

He looks at me, mouth gaping, at the police tape, at the immense hole in the road, the absent hillside, the total absence of Ma's house. He's not even hamming it up: he really can't speak.

He keeps looking from the hole to me and back again.

I raise my eyebrows at him, nod knowingly, and smile showing all my teeth, probably even the molars near the back I am smiling so broadly.

I see him take in the pale blue city water works truck that has joined the pair of police cruisers that remain on site, along with two white mini vans with circular orange and black "City of Baltimore" decals on their sides. I see him figure, as anyone could, how yesterday's big puddle became today's big hole. After all, Baltimore residents have been enjoying the drama of water and sewer related sink-holes for quite some time. A bunch of cars and most of a residential street had got sucked into one last year. The museum and historic Mount Vernon neighborhood are even now awkwardly barricaded by security walkways and temporary above ground pipelines because the whole area is perched on cement slabs a century old over massive sewers that have caved in and caused remarkably extensive, smelly, underground erosion.

Maybe a sink hole isn't such a surprise in Baltimore anymore. The fact that one entirely ate Ma's house is.

Eventually, after Tyrell has been speechless but slack jawed for some time, I cannot help myself and I start laughing again. I am so happy, so elated. I am bent over laughing, hands on my knees. Tyrell looks even more puzzled by my happiness, and this makes me laugh even harder.

Finally he spits out, "But we were just *there*. Not even a full day ago!"

After four days at Surrey Memorial, Will is moved to an in-patient drug rehabilitation facility in Jessup, one that only allows visitors on a select handful of days throughout the three month intensive rehab period.

At Surrey, I see Will every day. If I am not teaching yoga (painfully, with sore knees), I am there, with him. He is tranquilized that whole week; it is hard to have a conversation with him, but it seems clear he wants to go to Jessup for rehab.

"Pups, I gotta *go*. I *gotta*," he says in one not-lucid but still seemingly pertinent moment. "Everyone's dying out there. The dealers put fentanyl in everything, even weed! Get everyone hooked, don't tell. They don't tell when it's in. What it's in. Sell you horse, but it's just something powdery with fentanyl in it. So you don't know and then BOOM you're an OD. I gotta go to Jessup or I'll die."

So, he gets moved to Jessup and I know my first visiting day won't be until late November.

I am impressed through it all by how *smart* Will is being: he is getting off the streets to avoid the fentanyl epidemic (and he is going to avoid winter too if he plays it right: three months will take him to January and then there is an affiliated program which could provide housing and retraining in "life and work skills" for up to three months after that).

It's foresight, I think, and wonder if I am being disloyal somehow by suspecting it. Did he know, when he came to ask me for money, that he was going to use some of it for bus fare to get to Timonium? It seems very likely to me the whole Timonium "Merry Christmas" escapade was a performance, calculated, planned, and so *clever*. I admire Will's survival instinct. Grudgingly, I also admire that he never says to me that he wants to be clean, to stop using. He just doesn't want to die. He's addicted, but not suicidal.

I am exhausted by it all. It takes me several days to recover from my visits to Surrey Memorial, which means a little more than a week has passed from the night of the sinkhole before I am up to stopping in on Danny. I go to the market first and buy him an outrageous purple orchid and a "Congratulations!" card into which I scrawl, cryptically and I hope poetically "May you sink (your teeth) into something new now that all that's behind you!" Knowing that sometimes he sleeps a little late, I show up on his porch in the mid-afternoon, without Girlfriend or Blue, and with the orchid in a big paper bag to shield it from the cold bite in the afternoon wind. Danny greets me with huge smile:

"Em! Where the heck have you *been*? I've been by your house every day and you are always out. I have been making those poor dogs crazy."

It's so good to be at his house, to drink his tea (hot, black, honey-sweetened this afternoon) and to hear about his plans to make a different type of cookie for Christmas this year ("Thought I'd make a big ginger bread house and then invite you and Tyrell and some other folks over to break bits off until it's gone" he says, delighted with his own idea). I sink into the corner of his small couch and feel relaxed, happy.

Danny laughs at the card, and smiles about the orchid ("Ooo! *Exotic*"). He tells me that insurance won't pay him a dime for the loss of his Ma's house because he is not covered for any circumstance involving "earth moving" or flood damage. He's lucky, he claims, that the city admits some liability for the grey water damage and erosion otherwise he'd have to pay to fill the hole. As it stands, they will fill it, but not landscape the property or rebuild anything. It will take months. He's so cheerful as he tells me all this, as if it is all incredibly good news. It doesn't sound so great to me, but it's hard not to go along with Danny's good cheer. He tells me he has a job interview next week (as an accounts manager for an urban farm on Greenmount, near the cemetery), and that he went on one this week as well (as counter staff at Popeye's but they wouldn't hire him because he's too old).

"I'm looking for something different," he says. "Don't know what. Accounting is my main skill. That and my smile, of course. I like it when I brighten someone's day. Not sure what I can find. I am going to do just enough though Em," he says. "I don't want to work hard, just something steady. So I can buy groceries, you know? Maybe splash out a little and get health insurance."

I smile and nod: his plans sound less practical to me than Will's do. He sounds completely unrealistic, but he's *so happy* that I am certainly not going to burst his bubble. I wonder if any of the yoga studios want some accounting help? I could ask. I could see if I could find him something legit. I don't say any of this to Danny.

I do invite him to an event I think he'd enjoy. The yoga studio on Falls Road has invited a group of Buddhist monks, followers of the Dalai Lama, to come all the way from their monastery in India to make a peace mandala out of sand, and then tip it into the river. The idea is to teach non-attachment: make something beautiful, and then let it go. I invite Danny to the last day of the ceremony, the "releasing" of the mandala into the Jones Falls. All things considered, I think Danny and I will both get a kick out of it. Danny, already delighted with life, is enthusiastic.

"That sounds great, Em! Weird, a little, but great! Fun. Yes. Count me in."

DANNY

Em's invited me to a yoga-Buddhism thing. I don't know much about either, but I am excited: I feel like I can try new things these days. Somehow that feeling of carnival, of "well, all bets are off now!" has stuck with me. I feel like I am being flooded with newness like Ma's house got sucked under and flooded with water. I am just grinning and happy all the time. It's all new.

We get to the yoga place early so Em and I can see the Buddhist guys finish their art. The studio is just off Falls Road. Em drives. We park around the back of a nice-looking Mount Washington strip mall, between a take-out pizza place and a high-end sushi restaurant. Through the unremarkable glass doors is a lobby full of shoes. Em kicks off her boots, and looks at me, pointedly, until I remove my sneakers. I wish I'd known this part was coming: I bet my shoes stink.

We go through a pair of sliding doors into a large, dimly-lit room with gleaming wood floors. There are people in here but they are silent, seated on round cushions on the floor, cross-legged, backs military-straight. Near the front are the Buddhist monks, also cross-legged, seated in a square around the art they are making. There are five men, in deep red robes with golden egg-yolk yellow accents in the chest area. They are all wearing medical face masks, which surprises me until I see what they are doing: there are more than twenty little white bowls surrounding them, each with a different brightly colored powder, *sand* I remember, something about a *peace sand mandala*.

The masks must be so they don't breathe in the sand as they lean over their work. They've got metal tubes that narrow at the tip which they use to delicately, precisely, funnel colored sand into just the spot they want. The work, on a blue square panel on the floor between the men, maybe four feet by four feet, is incredibly detailed: There's a big circle of bright color, swirls of every shade of blue in one quadrant like an ornate sea, reds and oranges in another, like the monks's own clothes turned into an elaborate curlicue of color and pattern. At the center there's a blue bird in front of something that looks like a globe: that must be the peace part, doves, the world and all that.

Em whispers to me that this is the last day of a week-long series of chanting and mandala making sessions, intended to culminate in the destruction of their carefully crafted art. It's almost done. The monks are working on tiny empty areas in a piece that is predominantly rich swirls of color. Em tells me the idea is that in the making is beauty, in the artifact is beauty, and in the destruction or dissolution of that artifact is also beauty.

She has set a firm round cushion out for me and she sits, so I do too. When she sits cross-legged, her knees come to the floor and she looks like a comfortable pyramid (I guess the scabs must have stopped hurting). When I sit, my knees poke upwards, sharply, like the bent legs of a grasshopper. The monks continue their work in the quiet room, and the room continues to fill, with more people seating themselves silently around us. It's a peaceful crowd. I try not to look around too much; everyone else seems pretty focused on the Buddhists, or on their own palms cradled in their laps. I try not to shift around too much, even though the position makes my hips and knees feel weird.

Eventually, the Buddhist guys finish, and tidy up their tools and bowls, remove their masks. The mandala, intricate and bright, seems to shimmer. The five men arrange themselves behind the mandala, seated. They've put on some kind of headdresses, each wearing something like an elaborate rooster's coxcomb but bright yellow instead of red. Maybe they are supposed to look like sunlight? It startles me when they start chanting, their voices burbling somewhere between a bass guitar's lowest note repeatedly twanged and the big shiny bell-shaped bubbles one might emit from the floor of a swimming pool when trying to stay under. I notice that the monk closest to me is wearing white Hanes sport socks under his robes. I am wearing socks just like them. It makes me want to laugh; it reminds me that I am happy. These magical exotic men, they have ordinary feet just like me, and socks from Target.

The next, tricky, part is the careful lifting of the four

by four piece of blue plexiglass and the mandala upon it. The monks easily perform this task; I wonder how often they do it. Maybe they just tour the US; maybe they make dozens of sand mandalas a year? There's an awkward period in which people find and put on their shoes and add coats and sweaters to their outfits and then we all process out behind the monks (who wear, I notice, sport sandals over their Target socks), through the incongruously ordinary suburban parking lot to a shrubby area with a narrow dirt path which leads in turn to the river.

There must be fifty people trying to crowd around and see. The Jones Falls is shallow here, only about a foot or so deep, but wide and rocky. The water runs clear over the copper-hued rocks. There is more chanting, and then the square surface is tipped and sand begins mixing, begins cascading off the edge into the water, mingling in the clear flow, and sinking. One of the monks rings a bell over and over as this happens. It's mesmerizing to watch the sand tumble off the edge of the plastic, to watch it like a curtain of light falling, to watch the pattern disappear utterly.

I realize that I have been holding my breath while watching; I have been absorbed in this act like I am caught up in a suspense movie or something. I have been totally focused. As my focus shifts from falling sand back to myself, I am aware that Em, and a few other people, are staring at me. Why? What are they looking at? I realize I have been standing, mouth agape, not breathing, and that to see better I have moved forwards from the crowd. I have been standing in the river itself. My white sneakers are fully submerged, and the bottom six inches or so of my jeans are soaked. I realize, suddenly, that the water is surprisingly cold, that my toes are totally numb. The whole thing comes as a shock to me. I must look surprised. I certainly feel surprised. Em grins at me, and then starts laughing.

I look back to the where the mandala dissolved, and see that one of the monks is looking straight at me where I stand in the river. At first, it feels like being in a gun sight or something; I am at the narrow focus point of what he sees, and he looks just at me. I freeze, self-conscious, guilty.

It feels like he sees everything about me, but then I notice his soft eyes: it's actually a welcoming, understanding gaze. His gaze transforms me from a foolish spectacle upriver from his "real" event to an important, revealing part of the event itself. He smiles and laughs over the water, as if with Em who is also still laughing: it is a generous, kind laugh. And I laugh too, but I am also crying. Tears are running, streaming, from me to the river.

I want, suddenly and urgently, to be at Ma's. I want to stand with my feet at *that* boundary between solid ground and something other. I want to lay a stone there for Linnie.

Pull like gravity, back to me, to their right place.

Walker and thin man. He sees the light on the water; she sees the light on the water. The flicker of brightness over the dark catching one's eye and then the other's. Over the rocks flow the murmuring waters, the rapid current which runs through veins/ of porous earth. They cataract here, and into the trees these two, spiraling in, the walker and the thin man: sunny spots of greenery behind the parking lot. The dead child sunk into a deep down cavernous garden bright with sinuous rills.

Almost there.
Almost here.

The other lost one, the walker's brother-kin, white blond: He spins further and further up away from my earth, drunk on the milk of paradise.

Danny

I looked down that afternoon to see my feet in the frigid, bright river water and saw the rock: brownish, round, the size of a round loaf of bread, or of a small cat curled into a ball for sleeping. Its chubby brownness reminded me of Linnie, and now I'm on my porch with Tyrell holding the thing awkwardly on my thighs while trying to make a mark on it.

"My friend," said Tyrell, "looks like you are going to hurt yourself!"

I have a hammer in my right hand and in my left, a heavy eight inch road pin that I found up by Ma's house where part of the roadway is now a series of metal plates over a cavern. I am hitting the pin head with the hammer, trying to make a dent on the rock, and Tyrell is laughing.

"You are going to drive that thing into your leg, my friend, and then you'll have to explain *that* to the folks at the ER."

I'd had in mind carving "Linnie" on the rock, or, when I figured how hard the rock was, a simple elegant "L," but I am getting nowhere. I can't make a dent.

"Want me to give it a try?" Tyrell offers and I pass him the hammer, wordlessly.

"What you going for, here?"

"See if you can make a mark on that thing at all, and

then we can figure out what I am going for."

He stands up off his Home Depot bucket, takes the handsome, smooth stone from my knees, and grabs the pin. He sets the rock on the porch floor, braces it with his foot, picks up the pin to use as a chisel, steadies the pin and whacks forcefully with the hammer: Tyrell is surprisingly strong. There's a *chink* sound that sounds like what I imagine good masonry work is supposed to sound like and then a clatter as Tyrell accidentally loses his grip on the pin. The stone skips sideways over Tyrell's foot, as if to escape off the porch and down the street.

"You OK?" I ask

Tyrell is wincing: "O! Gonna have a bruise right in the arch of my foot! I guess I need to wear work-boots if I am going to spend time on your porch, huh?"

He picks up the rock with both hands, looks at it, laughs, and hands it to me.

There's a small circular puncture in the smooth surface of the rock, and, I guess because of the skip, another, slightly less deep, right next to it. The pair look like an umlaut.

"'S good," I say, "Let's go."

Tyrell looks confused. He doesn't know about Linnie-in-the-attic of the house that's now in a big hole. He doesn't know about her umlaut.

"It's enough." I say emphatically, "It's the right kind of mark."

"O-K" he says, sarcastically, and then, more lightly, "Glad my craftsmanship meets your needs today, *sir!*"

"Let's go." I repeat.

It is the eerie half-light of fall evening. The sky is purplish, the buildings and trees are almost silhouettes having lost most, but not quite all of their color to the dimming light. We walk to Ma's. There is still security tape around most of the area, with just a narrow strip of road usable over the steel plates that tip, tilt and clang alarmingly when one walks over them. On the north side there's an entry road of sorts to what has become a worksite, with cement trucks coming during the day to pour their contents into the depths of the earth. It's quiet here now though. I am holding the rock, bare in my hands. I have no bag or anything with me. Tyrell and I just walked off the porch as we were. I skirt the tape, alongside the remaining neighbor's house on the south side: I know it is empty now, residents evacuated until the area is deemed stable and safe. Closer to the chasm on this side of things is a chain link fence festooned in "Danger! Keep Out!" signs. I get as close as I can, right up to the chain, and I can see the chasm is about ten feet in from the other side of the fence.

"Stand with me a sec." I ask Tyrell. Wordlessly, he does. He's looking at the hole. I am looking at the stone in my hands. I take some deep breaths. I feel the stone heavy, smooth in my two hands. I close my eyes and try to remember what Linnie weighed. As I breathe in I smell a fresh cool soil smell of early evening, of plants exhaling their fresh green oxygen in the last bit of day. The insides of my eyelids sparkle like the light off the river earlier today.

I want a solemn feeling, but I hear the monk's happy laughter instead. I can feel Tyrell's puzzlement emanating from him. One more deep breath and I try and think "rest in peace" for Linnie but instead I get Tyrell starting to laugh. He's trying to hold it in, but he can't. I shoot him a fierce look.

"Sorry, sorry," he chokes "I don't why. It's funny! You. One rock! It's not going to fill the hole, man." Laughing.

"It's not to fill the hole!" I am irritated, but in spite of myself I feel myself catching his laughter: "It's to lay it all to rest. Memorial of sorts." I say, by way of inadequate explanation. Tyrell nods, breathless with giggles.

Both hands on the rock, I turn sideways to swing it backwards like a wrecking ball and then forwards, releasing to let it launch upwards, hoping it will make it to the pit. I imagine it landing on the level ground and not going into the hole at all. That would be disappointing, embarrassing. What would I do? Climb the fence? Kick it in? Or stay put on this side of the fence, impotent, and just leave it there? The smooth stone flies high though, a dark silhouetted orb describing an elegant, stately arc through the sky's deepening purple. It goes up, and then speeds downwards. It disappears soundlessly past the lip of the hole. I wait, holding my breath to hear it hit the bottom, but I hear nothing. It's like the stone just keeps flying downwards forever.

Bear

Ursa Major in the crystalline dark heavens. In spring she padded softly into the firmament. The seven hunters pursue her, all summer long. Four of them, Pigeon, Horned-Owl, Blue-Jay and Saw-whet have given up now, have laid themselves to nest and sleep and rest below the horizon. Three lean closer in, ardent on her trail: Moose Bird, Chickadee and closest to her, the strongest, Robin.

The Great Bear sees their increasing intent on her. She knows, she always knows, what will come again this year as it always has.

She rears up, pawing the night:

"Robin, Chickadee, Moose Bird, I am not afraid of your arrows."

The hunters's eyes sparkle bright in the crisp darkness. They are afraid; They do not respond.

"I am not afraid." The bear stands tall on two legs, immense, and roars it, swinging her great skull at them, her teeth blue-white in the night. The winds shudder.

It is time. Robin looses his arrow in a great anxious flutter.

His arrow will enter the great bear through her open mouth, staving her very tongue, stilling her growls and bravery, running down her throat to her heart and stopping the strong pulse.

Her blood will spatter forth. A great gout, hot and

dark, will rebound over Robin. Robin will find himself drenched in the thickness of it and be terrified. He will shake, and flap. The great bear's blood will rain and the tree leaves so far below will flush purple-red with it. Her blood will make the leaves wither and fall.

Robin will run away, the red of the great bear still warm on his heart.

Chickadee and Moose Bird will gorge themselves, will pick the bear clean till she is a skeleton.

Her bright constellation of bones will continue to step through the night sky. Cold. The blood drained from her.

Em

November. Time, finally, to visit Will. Visiting day is on a Friday. I have to get two of my yoga classes covered so that I can have the whole stretch of time, early morning through mid afternoon, available. The day comes with an itinerary, which the rehab center has forwarded me in an email attachment and which I have printed out: eight to nine-thirty coffee and cookies; nine-thirty to ten-thirty, tour of facility; ten-thirty to twelve-thirty, individual meetings with counsellors/ free time (my "individual meeting" is from eleven thirty to eleven forty-five, apparently); then lunch, then closing presentation of center goals. Wrap up by three.

I lay out my clothes the night before, in case I am sleepy in the morning, but then I hardly sleep. The dreams have stopped, the ones with Danny's Mom and Linnie. They stopped right after the sinkhole, but I have been having trouble sleeping at all since then, since Will went into rehab. On this night, I conk out at ten, but wake up, fully, at two in the morning and spend the next hours forcing my eyes closed, not sleeping. Before dawn, I shut the alarm off before it rings, get dressed, walk the dogs (Sherwood gardens route: it is cold and we are up early so we don't run into any other dogs, just a lone, huffing jogger in the dark), make tea which I don't drink and toast which I don't eat. Jessup is out past the airport, so I leave at seven just in case the traffic is bad.

The traffic is bad, and it takes me a full hour before I get to the center, carefully following the directions I have handwritten down, even though my phone could tell me the way if I felt like listening to a disembodied woman's voice politely insist on which exits I need to take and when. Her voice stresses me out. It makes me make wrong turns, some sort of perverse reflex rejection of her imperatives. I park in front of what looks like a handsome brick colonial style home and go to the front door. I ring the bell at the front door and am greeted by a young woman with a clipboard:

"Goodness! Is it that time already?" she asks, patting her apron pocket to find a ball point pen. "Name?"

"Em Fletcher."

She scans the list and then pauses "Ah." Looks at me, looks back at the list, takes a deep breath, all of which makes me nervous, and then "Please follow me. We're going to settle *you* in the office for a moment, OK?"

The office is to the left of the front door. The hall here is carpeted in something faux-Persian. It's a homey deep red, though threadbare from much traffic and cleaning.

I am invited to sit on a loveseat that backs up to the window, facing a large wooden desk. I sit, and wait. I look at the desk, its computer, the landscape painting hanging on the wall behind it (a mountain meadow, full of bright flowers with a white-capped craggy mountain in the distance). My back is to the window, but I can hear the young woman answer the door to other people, presumably other visitors, and usher them into some deeper part of the building. It's just me who has to wait in the office, apparently. I worry that something has happened to Will. I fidget my hands around a napkin I find in my coat pocket. My stomach grumbles; I could do with some of the coffee and cookies the schedule promised I would be getting at this hour.

Eventually an older woman with short-cropped hair and an unfashionable peach satin blouse enters: "Hello. I am Jane Williams, the event planner. Our counsellor and our manager aren't in yet. They will be at nine-thirty if you want to wait."

"Uh. OK. Is everything OK?"

"Oh yes! Yes, Ma'am. Everything is fine."

"My brother Will?"

"Oh" Jane looks towards the door with consternation "Did Ila not say when she brought you in?" She kisses her teeth, scolding young Ila in her absence: "Will changed his mind. He said he doesn't want any visitors today. He says he isn't up to it just yet."

I wait for an hour, and the counsellor comes to tell me the same thing with no more explanation than Jane provided. I can hear the happy hubbub of visitors in the building, and I know Will is back there somewhere, and that he has chosen not to see me. He doesn't want to see *me.*

I go home.

The dogs greet me at the door, wagging and barking. Blue jumps up, launching upwards to lick my face but missing and thumping me in the nose, hard. It hurts. I wipe my thumb under my nostrils and my hand comes away bloody. The dogs are still barking and I start to yell.

"Shut the fuck up! Would you just. Fuck. Off. Shut up!"

Blue cowers for a moment, and then bursts up, wagging and squirming, trying to greet me. He barks again, loudly.

"Urghhhh!" I cover my ears against the barking, see the blood drip from my nose to the floor. "Urghhhh!"

Blue and Girlfriend don't react to my anger or my bleeding. They carry on, claws scratching on the hard floor as they scamper and cavort. It makes me even more frustrated, the fact that even on them *I have no impact.*

"Get out!" I yell, gesticulating towards the kitchen and the back door, and then tromping awkwardly through the house to let them out: "Go! Now!"

The dogs pause a moment to look at me, puzzled.

"Go!"

Blue pivots back towards the living room and makes a play bow with a deep snarl of pleasure. Girlfriend leaps to him, front paws flat-smacking the floor just by his shoulder where he's crouched. She's yipping happily in high excitement. The noise of their snarling and yipping and joy, it's like being inside a garbage compactor.

"Ughhhhh!" Frustrated at the dogs that won't go out, I step outside myself instead, and shut the door behind me. *Damn fucking dogs.* I can still hear their raucous playing, but it is quieter out here. A squirrel is chittering over something. The afternoon shadows are cast long and dark across the lawn. My nose has got blood spatters on my jeans, and my hands look like I have been doing some rough country surgery on someone: blood is smeared and drying dark into all the knuckle lines. You can see a dark blood trail where I have repeatedly wiped my nose with my right hand, all along my forefinger.

The shadow of the house roof reaches all the way to the hollow in the yard's corner where Will and I used to hide, the roof part of the shadow looking like an arrow. The hollow isn't really visible, but if you knew it was there, you'd know the house was pointing to it.

In Mid-December, despite my rocky start at the greenhouse and the ongoing delays at Ma's property, I host my bake-in. I don't care that my house is small, and my kitchen too. I *want* it to be crowded; I want it to be fun. I invite Tyrell, and his daughter with her kids and her man. I invite Cee, Ma's neighbor, the woman I was in grade one with. I've been bumping into her a lot these days, heading up to the Big Hole and back. I check on the city's progress every couple of days. They've poured a bunch of concrete down there, but the fill hasn't arrived yet. Might not come until the new year, apparently.

I invite some of the folks I know from the Greenmount farm, even though I've only been doing their accounts, office work and ordering for a month: two young guys with Buddy Holly glasses and enormous beards. One is Mike and the other is Sean. Sean is younger, redder, and maybe a bit slimmer. He works with the hydroponic lettuces. Mike is a bit chubbier. At the greenhouse, he's got indoor strawberries struggling and spindly in the winter chill that he's trying to make fruit in time for Valentine's day. They dress the same, and those big beards: I often am not sure which one I am looking at if I come into a room and only one of them is in there. They've both been patient with me: accounts I am good at, greenhouse gardening not at all, *yet*. There's been a bit of a learning curve for me.

Frankly, it's not just that I am new to organic hydroponic farming. It's been a good long time since I've lived in the culture of a forty hour work week, and, it is true, some mornings I look at myself in the bathroom mirror and wonder if it really would be so bad to just go back to bed, maybe forever. There are some bad days in all of this effort to remake myself. Some days that old weight is still heavy in me. Ma's house is gone, but it didn't take all my memories with it.

I am also new to the urban renewal that the farm represents.The Greenmount neighborhood had been among the worst for poverty, violent crime and gang activity. Now there's all of this upper-middle-class, suburban money pouring in to revitalize it. The greenhouses are flanked by a cemetery full of white folks who ranked highly in the civil war, a new "maker space" called Open Works where community members can buy a membership and use community owned carpentry, 3-D imaging and sewing workshop space, and a tool library.

History (the civil war era), the recent past (poverty, crime) and the present (well -intentioned and ostensibly community focused development) all rub cheeks here. What are we all supposed to be making with the tools at Open Works and the Tool Library? Houses? Or art?

At the greenhouse, we are making produce. Clean, fresh, sold right out of our own door to people who can buy with WIC (Women, Infants and Children Nutrition support, kind of like food stamps). Greenmount is in a food desert (there are no grocery stores in walking distance), so a lot of our WIC customers have bizarre diets poised between bodega and macrobiotic: chips and organic microgreens, rice a roni with heirloom Cherokee purple tomatoes and scarlet runner beans. At the café in Open Works you can buy "transparently traded" coffee and steamed organic milk from a dairy in Pennsylvania in Italiante combinations like cortado or cappuccino.

Also from the greenhouse I've invited a woman named LaQuesha. She wears a tight red kerchief on her hair and her big curves are accentuated by the low-buttoned men's shirts she likes to wear tucked into her high-waisted jeans. She's got bright red lipstick and a chunky man's watch.

I invite my Coldspring neighbors: a young woman with her two babies from one side, and two men who live with their disabled brother from the other. The brother is a biggish guy in a wheelchair. It was a production getting him up my front steps—lots of lifting and yelling and too many hands helping—but now he's in his chair, parked by my front door, watching out the window and back to the kitchen, looking happy as long as I keep giving him ice cubes to suck. I invite Em, and her friend Bev and even Bev's friend Mary who is today wearing a vivid pumpkin-colored turtle-neck sweater and fashionably close-cropped dark hair.

The party starts at three in the afternoon. There's no liquor, just a lot of hot tea. There's an enormous mess on the counter and kitchen table—gingerbread fixings and tools for its shaping, bowls and spoons dirty in the sink, crumbs and dough on the floor. It's loud. It smells overwhelmingly of baked allspice and ginger, the air thick with it. Panels of gingerbread on baking trays (I had to buy extra trays) come out of the oven and get set out on the porch to cool: Tyrell's job is to smoke cigarettes and to guard them until they are firmed up, then they get brought back inside.

Bev and Mary, and Sean/Mike from Greenmount are letting Nyasha's kids assemble the pieces, or rather, the grown-ups are assembling the pieces while carefully preserving for the children the impression that the children are assembling the pieces. There's white icing all over the coffee table, and sticky white fingerprints at child height all over the walls in the living room. The gingerbread house that's coming together is huge.

Em shows up late. She finds me inside, gives me a hug:

"Sorry I'm late. I made something for your gingerbread house," lifting the lid of a Tupperware container. At first I don't know what I am looking at: brown splotches carefully separated with leaves of wax paper. I guess I look puzzled enough that Em has to explain: "Chocolate squirrels! I made them myself."

"Ha! I see it now" And I look at her grey eyes: we've

never talked about how she knows all those things. I certainly never *told* her about Ma and me worrying about the squirrels disturbing things in the attic. And yet here they are, squirrels, and I am guessing it's a joke Em's making based exactly on those unspoken details of my childhood.

"'S'OK, right?" she asks, hopefully.

I put an arm round her shoulder, give her a peck on the cheek: "Better than OK. Funny, and thoughtful." I add, quickly, while I've got her close, "You see Will yet?"

"Nah," she looks away, eyes instantly tearing up. "Nah. He still doesn't want to see me."

When it is done, the ginger bread house stands about three feet tall, with a steep gabled roof surprisingly *like* Ma's place. It's decorated with peppermints, jujubes and jelly beans all glued on with white icing. Even though the house is huge, Em's chocolate squirrels still aren't to the right scale: they are too big. There are eight of them, menacingly large, on the roof and sides of the house. They crack me up. They are as big, maybe, as they once were in my imagination.

LaQuesha has brought a proper camera, with a zoom lens. It hangs around her neck on a sturdy black strap, nestles heavily between her large breasts. She asks us to pose behind the gingerbread:

"Group shot!" she calls, but as folks start to gather in the cramped living room she realizes we aren't all going to fit in there at once.

"OK, OK. First all the wise ones" and she shepherds the kids in, and, grinning at her own mischief, a reluctant-looking but delighted Cee.

"Now the artists!" and she scoots the wheel-chair in, and gets Mike/Sean, Bev, Mary and Tyrell's daughter Nyasha to stand with him.

She calls one odd grouping after another giving them all unexpected and maybe prophetic titles: The Dreamers, Shake and Bake, the Life of the Party, the Best Appetites. She takes dozens of photos, with candid shots—people laughing, moving, making funny faces with each other—in-between. It's good. Her staging gets us all moving around and talking, even to the people we don't know.

"Mmmmm. One last one." LaQuesha announces.

"You" (plucking Tyrell's sleeve)

"and *you*" (trailing her finger flirtatiously along the whole length of bewildered-looking Em's arm) and, she pauses, casting her eye around the room, landing on me and then announcing, as if surprised at her own choice:

"You! The host with the most. The Prime Numbers, the Mover-Shakers? Nah. You guys are Govans Gothic. Get it? Like the painting!"

"But there are *three* of us?" Em stammers.

Tyrell looks confused.

LaQuesha waves, flaps and ushers until Tyrell and Em flank me and we stand behind the gingerbread. We smile.

"Terrible!" announces LaQuesha. "Quit smiling!"

So Tyrell ducks down, clowning, to squat behind the house with his arms outstretched, making it look like *it* has hands, I grab the broom and stand it bristles-up between Em and me. We pull long faces. LaQuesha snaps. The result, when we view it on the tiny screen on the back of LaQuesha's camera is, as intended, a weird kind of parody of American Gothic. I love it. I get out my new Kyocera "stupid" phone (a crappy blackberry knock-off, with no internet browsing features, years out of date before I even bought it) so I can enter LaQuesha's number, and text her so she has mine. I want a copy of the photo.

Em wants one too. She gets her phone out. LaQuesha's eyes are locked onto Em. I make an excuse to go back to the kitchen. When I look over several minutes later, LaQuesha's still talking to Em, and the two of them are laughing.

Later, I tell everyone to crack off a big chunk of gingerbread and candy, to break it all up, to take some home.

RELEASE

Frost but no snow. Worms, beetles burrowed deep and still to sleep through the cold months. The skeleton of the great bear bright and slender in the sky, the bones of the child white and crumbling at the root of her mother's house under a love-stone, under a knit-together of short-mortal friendship, under the dead cold calm of the watching timeless sky.

Still earth, waiting.

Along the York Road neon lights twinkle in the darkness: human, terrestrial, a low-slung night constellation. Street lights red green amber for the cars that do not pass in a still hour of human sleep.

A static ease.
A cold calm.
Stone over heart.
Well-achieved.

Release it like a snake of breath-mist in the frigid tight dark.

It's early morning but dark out, and cold. February is the coldest winter month, always. I am awake well before I need to be. Blue is curled behind my knees, a heavy dead weight that has given me cramps in my calves. I reach down to stroke him gently, grateful that he is there.

The dogs groan when I get up, follow me reluctantly downstairs. Neither asks to go out: Blue flops down on the rug, Girlfriend makes herself small and circular in the crook of the sofa. I stand in the kitchen with the light off, planning to make tea but not quite getting to it, admiring the full-bellied purple eggplant on the counter: a gift from LaQuesha, from the greenhouse. Next to it, a notepad with the name and phone number Bev gave me: the great therapist in Owings Mills. In red ink below are the date and time of my first appointment.

I look out the kitchen window. The streetlight in the alley has cast a greyish light over the backyard. I can see frost in the grass. With a start, I realize I can see someone standing in the far corner, back to me, standing on the edge of the depression out there. It's the height of Will, the shape of Will.

My breath catches. I want to go out to him, but I know that if he wanted to see me he would have knocked on the door. He didn't. I watch Will stand there, back to me, looking down at the hiding place we so often shared as children. I can see the cloud his warm breath makes in the cold dark. Abruptly, briefly, he turns to look at the house, as if he sees something in one of my upstairs windows, and then, lumbering, not agile but moving like an old man, a heavy man, he awkwardly clambers over my chain link fence, and walks away down the alley.

Acknowledgements

While the characters in my work are fictional, this part of northern Baltimore city, its history, and many of its historical figures are not. Of particular use to me in my research were: John Bain's *Govans Village and Suburb*, Dorothy Worsham Earp's *Govans as I Remember it*, Lee McCardell's *A History of Govans*, Rebuilding Baltimore's *Woodbourne McCabe: A Brief History* and Thomas Scharf's *History of Baltimore City and County*. The Maryland Historical Society was a key source for historic maps and information on Elizabeth Patterson Bonaparte. I was inspired by Mr. Donald (not that Donald) formerly at 406 E. Coldspring Lane, may he rest in peace. I also have to thank my student Oonagh Kligman for introducing me to Boltzmann, the website *Susquehannock History*, and Mary Kunaniec Skeen who was willing to talk to me about her experiences living in this area from the 1970s through to the present day.

Mary was introduced to me by Juniper Ellis, whose feedback on the earliest versions of this text was invaluable. Madison Smartt Bell provided the encouragement, the professional skill, and the publishing advice required to bring this manuscript to completion. Also thanks to readers Dan Marcus and Flo Martin.

The romantic sublime permeates this work, sometimes in the phrasings of writers like Keats, Coleridge or even (though modernists) Yeats and Eliot. There are smatterings too of American transcendentalism and dim echoes of Thoreau.

Antje M. Rauwerda was raised in Canada, Singapore, North Wales, Texas, and Ghana. She makes her home in Baltimore city with her teenagers and her dogs. She is a Professor of British and Postcolonial Literatures at Goucher College.

9 781959 556893